A Question of Love

Sequel to A Question of Trust.

A past with three, a future for two...

Gabe Carter and his best friend Connor's passion for threesomes brought Tina Jenkins into Gabe's bed—and into his heart. As a matter of honor, he gave up the woman he loved. Time passes, times change and old promises fall away, but Gabe is still in love with Tina. Now he's going after his heart's desire.

Tina has her own opinion about Gabe's sense of honor. His departure tore apart the most special of bonds and destroyed her relationship with Connor, leaving her brokenhearted. It took her a long time to pick up the pieces, a struggle she doesn't wish to repeat. When Gabe shows up at her favorite coffee shop, she knows just where to tell him to stick his apology.

Gabe isn't so easily put off—and Tina can't help but respond to his seduction. Picking up where they left off is tempting, but Gabe wants her all to himself. And Tina wants the whole package, which includes Connor.

At the risk of crushing his hopes for the future, Gabe sets out to prove he's more than enough man for her...

Warning: If piping hot sex, ménage scenes, adult toys, anal play, short blonde heroines and stacked, muscular heroes are not your cup of tea, then don't read this book. You won't enjoy it.

Going All In

The higher the stakes, the harder they fall—in love.

Julia Savage's weekly poker games are tearing her apart. She's in love with two of her fellow card players, and much as she'd like to pick and confess her true feelings to one man, she won't. Not if it means risking the love of the other.

Hunter Miles has wanted Julia for four months, and he's about to deal a hand she couldn't see coming. He's determined to give her a New Year's Eve celebration she never expected. He's going to seduce her—in front of his friend and rival for her affections, Jay Baxter. But Jay's not willing to lay down his cards. He's going after Julia too, and he's not above bluffing to get what he wants. Either way, one of them is going to win her over.

Unless they change the rules of the game. If they double up, there's a chance they can split the pot...

Warning: This book contains two hunky heroes, a heroine worth betting on, sizzling hot three-way action (m/f/m and m/m/f), a whole lot of unexpected fireworks and a New Year's Eve to remember.

Look for these titles by
Jess Dee

Now Available:

Ask Adam
Photo Opportunity
A Question of Trust
A Question of Love
Winter Fire

Circle of Friends Series
Only Tyler
Steve's Story

Three Of A Kind Series
Going All In
Raising The Stakes
Full House

Print Anthology
Three's Company

Risking It All

Jess Dee

SAMHAIN
PUBLISHING

Samhain Publishing, Ltd.
577 Mulberry Street, Suite 1520
Macon, GA 31201
www.samhainpublishing.com

Risking It All
Print ISBN: 978-1-60928-068-0
A Question of Love Copyright © 2011 by Jess Dee
Going All In Copyright © 2011 by Jess Dee

Editing by Jennifer Miller

This book is a work of fiction. The names, characters, places, and incidents are products of the writer's imagination or have been used fictitiously and are not to be construed as real. Any resemblance to persons, living or dead, actual events, locale or organizations is entirely coincidental.

A Question of Love, ISBN 978-1-60504-824-6
First Samhain Publishing, Ltd. electronic publication: November 2009
Going All In, ISBN 978-1-60504-852-9
First Samhain Publishing, Ltd. electronic publication: December 2009
First Samhain Publishing, Ltd. print publication: January 2011

Contents

A Question of Love

Dedication

With thanks to:

Everyone who read and critiqued this book to make it better – My indispensable Ozcritters and my fellow Samhellions, Viv Arend and Sami Lee.

Jennifer Miller, my brilliant editor.

And as always... My boys!

Chapter One

"Regular long black?"

Gabe Carter turned to the counter to accept his take-away coffee. As he did so, movement across the coffee shop caught his eye. A man stood, leaned over and brushed his mouth against that of a woman still sitting at the table. Their lips met, held, held some more and then some more.

She pulled away. The man waved and walked out of the coffee shop. The woman slumped back in her seat.

Gabe stared, stunned all the way down to his toes. His heart beat uneasily against his ribs. Goddamn. It couldn't be.

Could it?

'Course it could. Made sense too. The coffee shop on the corner. The same one where she and he and Connor Regan, his closest mate, had always hung out, every Sunday morning like clockwork. Wasn't that the reason he'd come here? Not for the coffee but for the memories? For the hope, the slight hope that maybe, just maybe, she would be here?

She hadn't been home, and the voice message on her mobile phone had informed him the number had been disconnected. Visiting the café had been a last desperate attempt to find her. Frustration needled his gut. Why had it taken him so long to come to his senses? Why the fuck hadn't he acted four years ago, when he'd realized just how deep his feelings ran for Tina Jenkins? He wouldn't have needed to track her down now.

Gabe shook his head to clear it. That didn't matter anymore. She was here. With a man, no less. *Fuck.* Was it the same man?

She hadn't changed, although her blonde hair was short now, cut in pixie-like wisps to frame her delicate face. She wrinkled her nose as she stared at her cup. Her almond-shaped eyes narrowed, and her mouth drooped in a despondent pout. A sexy despondent pout.

Arrows of apprehension struck his spine. Now what? He'd come searching for her, and he'd found her. Kissing someone. Did he do what instinct dictated? Stride towards her, kicking chairs out of his path, and haul her up in his arms? Carry her out of this place like a barbarian intent on claiming his woman? Prove that no other man was good enough for her?

Or did he acknowledge his crushing disappointment and her obvious status—still taken—and get the hell out of here?

Gabe took a sip of his coffee, hot, bitter and black, just the way he liked it, and made a decision. He was drinking Tina's favorite drink in Tina's favorite coffee bar. He'd come here to find her, and here she was. The very least he owed her, he owed himself, was a hello. What did he stand to lose?

Nothing. He'd already lost it all four years ago when he voluntarily walked away. Voluntarily left Sydney—and Tina— without looking back.

Gabe made his way through the small maze of tables, never once taking his gaze off her. Tina added a heaped teaspoon of sugar to her mug. Then another. She stirred her drink and shifted in her seat. She lifted the mug to her lips, took a sip, puckered her mouth in distaste and put the drink back down, pushing it far away.

The short hair suited her. It highlighted her high cheekbones and full mouth and made her lips look more kissable than ever. From five-odd meters away, above the strong aroma of fresh roasted coffee beans, he fancied he could smell her perfume. Sweet and intoxicating, like flowers from an exotic, tropical island. God, he'd always loved the way her scent had curled through his nose and hit him straight in the gut.

Her sigh reached his ears at the same time he reached her table. The downward slouch of her shoulders tugged at his heart. "You feeling sad, T?"

Tina's head shot up. Her eyes widened and her mouth dropped open, displaying glimpses of white teeth and a very pink, very tasty-looking tongue. Gabe almost groaned out loud at the thought of all the places that tongue had been. He almost groaned louder thinking of the man who'd just left and all the ways he must have enjoyed that tongue.

She gaped at him for several seconds, an array of emotions washing over her face. Then she sat up straight, narrowed her eyes and nodded coolly. "Well, well, well, if it isn't the disappearing man."

The ice in her voice slashed through his skin, and the cynicism in her words burned like salt on the fresh wound. He had no choice but to absorb the pain and do his best to ignore it. He'd come this far. There was no point in turning back now. "This seat taken?" He held the back of the recently vacated wooden chair.

Tina glanced at the door her male friend had walked through, hesitated, then shrugged. "Not anymore."

Gabe couldn't help himself. He checked out her left hand and nearly sagged in relief to find it unadorned by any rings. "Mind if I sit?"

"It's a free world."

What had he expected? That she'd take one look at him and melt in a puddle at his feet? Throw her arms around him and beg him to take her home?

Sure he'd hoped, but he hadn't expected.

"You're looking good, T," he said as he sat down. "Sad, but good." Okay, so right at this moment she looked more pissed off than sad. Didn't mean he hadn't seen the misery in her face as she'd watched the man—her man—walk away.

"What are you doing here, Gabe?"

Ah, she still had that feisty directness he'd found so arousing. "Grabbing a coffee. You?"

"Having a bubble bath," she bit out. "What does it look like I'm doing?"

She'd always had a sarcastic nature. It was one of the many things he liked about her. Her quick-witted, acidic comebacks were a reflection of her sharp mind. A low hum of desire vibrated deep in Gabe's stomach. He should have expected it. There'd never been a time with Tina when the hum had been absent.

He couldn't resist dropping his tone a notch. "I've seen you in a bubble bath. Doesn't look anything like what you're doing here."

She froze, the memory clear in her eyes. A long minute passed. Maybe two.

The bath hovered in his mind. Images of Tina, younger but no more innocent, submerged in its hot, soapy depths teased him, sending the blood in his veins rushing south.

Thousands of tiny white bubbles hid her arms and her legs. The only visible parts of her luscious flesh were the peaks of her breasts—the rosy, tight nipples that burst through the soap.

"So tell me, T, what's got you so sad?"

She bristled. "I'm fine, Gabe. Nothing has got me...sad."

He sat on the edge of the bath. Connor lounged against the wall of the shower. Tina's eyes were closed, her lips parted.

"You've got that look on your face. The one that tells me something is very wrong. Want to talk about it?"

"With you?" She gave a surprised snort. "Mr. I-won't-talk-unless-I-have-a-gun-pointed-at-my-head Carter? What do you want me to do, Gabe? Spill my heart while you sit there in your usual catatonic state?"

It took Gabe a couple of seconds to respond. Her words sliced through him, one by one, each syllable a dagger in his fast-failing confidence. "Sometimes it's good just to have someone listen. Someone who doesn't talk or pass judgment." It was her sentiment, not his, that he repeated now. She'd told him so one day when he'd held her and let her weep in his arms. Funny, he couldn't remember the reason she'd been crying, but he recalled her telling him she found his silence comforting.

She looked contrite. "I'm sorry. I shouldn't have said that."

Gabe shrugged, pretending a nonchalance he did not feel. "You're upset. I'm here. Easy enough to take it out on me."

Tina stared across the table at her drink.

"Whatever you do, fellas, don't leave now."

Gabe had no intention of going anywhere.

Neither, it appeared, did Connor. "There a reason you want us here, T?" Connor asked.

She looked at them both and grinned. "There sure is, boys. I want to watch you as you watch me touch myself. I want to see your faces when I come."

"Was there something you wanted, Gabe?"

Not much. Just to tell her he loved her and he had since

17

the first time he'd laid eyes on her. "To say hello. It's been a while."

She nodded, but refused to meet his gaze. "Hello."

Christ, she looked miserable. And angry. And beautiful. "You cut your hair." Maybe if he spoke about the mundane things, she'd relax a little.

She lifted her eyebrows. "Over a year ago."

"It looks good. Suits you."

"Thank you."

Beneath all those luxurious bubbles, hidden from view, Tina had her hand buried in her pussy. The knowledge was all it took to get Gabe hard again.

Water rippled around her breasts. A soft hiss escaped her mouth.

Connor stood a little straighter.

"How's your sister?" he asked. Ugh. Her sister. The last time he'd seen her she'd told him off something good.

"She's okay." Her gaze lifted to his chest.

Better than staring at her drink, he decided. "She still with that guy? Michael?" The two of them had warned Gabe to stay the hell away from Tina.

"You could say. They're married."

"They are? Congratulations." They'd been protecting Tina. It was unfair to hold it against them forever.

She smiled at his chest. A poor excuse for a smile, but a smile nevertheless. "I'm an aunt now."

"Niece or nephew?"

"Nephew. Jay is nine months."

"And spoiled rotten by you, I assume?"

She nodded. "You assume right."

"It feels good, fellas," Tina moaned. *"Real good."* She cupped a breast with her hand.

"What are you doing under there, T?" Connor asked, his voice a tone lower than usual.

She smiled at Connor. *"I'm touching myself. Playing with my...clit. Mmmmm."* Her eyes drifted shut. *"Pretending my hand is yours, C." She licked her lips,* sighed again, circled her nipple with her thumb. *"And you, Gabe... You're stroking my breast. Licking it with your tongue. Ooooh...hot!"*

At least they were talking now. He let his gaze wander until he caught sight of the sketch pad beside her chair. "You still at the firm?" he asked her.

She nodded.

"Still working for the old man?"

Tina frowned, looked him in the eye, nodded again and dropped her gaze.

Christ, what was she still doing there? Why hadn't she given up her secretarial job and done what she'd always wanted to do? Sketch full time. "How's your drawing coming along?"

She scowled at him. "Sketching," she corrected, like he knew she would. It had always driven her mad when he used the wrong term. "And it's coming along okay."

"Had your first exhibition yet?" Her lifelong dream had been to display her work in a public gallery.

"No."

He stared at her, shocked. "Why not?"

She shrugged. "Not good enough, I suppose."

He almost growled at her preposterous comment. "That's bullshit." She was a genius with a pencil. A true master of her art. Gabe had several of her framed sketches hanging on the walls in his office. His physical therapy patients never failed to

19

comment on their brilliance. He also had one he kept in a drawer beside his bed. That one was not for public scrutiny. "You're exceptional, and you know it."

Steam billowed around her. Her cheeks were stained a deep red. One nipple poked out beneath her fingers, hard and tight.

"I've moved my hand lower. Between my legs now. So...wet. Not like the water though." She swallowed. The bubbles rippled around her. "Mmmmm..."

Gabe's body temperature shot up ten degrees, at least.

She looked him in the eye. "What is this, Gabe? You trying to play catch up in five minutes?"

No. He'd have liked to play catch up for the rest of their lives. Not so easy considering the guy who'd had his tongue stuck halfway down her throat five minutes ago. "It's been a while, T. I'm happy to see you. Is it a crime to find out how you've been?"

"You know what, G?" There was nothing affectionate about her use of his old nickname. "I'm not interested. I don't want to discuss how I've been with you. I don't care how long we haven't seen each other for. In fact, I don't feel like chatting with you at all."

"God, fellas, that feels so damn good." Her breath came in sharp, short gulps. She hooked a foot over the edge of the bath. Water dripped to the floor.

She turned her head and looked at Connor. "My finger...imagining it's you...your cock..." She moaned.

Connor swore under his breath.

Gabe rubbed the back of his neck, trying to ease the cold prickles of her stinging words. "Ouch."

"Aw, did I offend you?" The sarcasm was back. "Sorry, sweetheart. I feel terrible. Really terrible." She grabbed her bag and hung it on her shoulder. "Now, if you'll excuse me, I have to go." Tina stood up. "It's been swell, G. Maybe we can do it again sometime. In, oh, I don't know, a year or four?"

And she left. Slung her bag over her shoulder, clutched her sketch pad at her side and walked right out the coffee shop without a backward glance, leaving him staring at her departing backside.

"Only...one thing...missing..." Her nut-brown eyes were wild when they met Gabe's, lust-filled and hazy.

Blood roared in his ears.

"You," she panted. "Missing you. Want...to...taste you."

She pulled her hand away from her breast and brought it to her chin. Her lips parted, and she sucked her index finger deep into her wet mouth.

Gabe forgot to breathe as Tina's back arched. Her breasts thrust through the bubbles, and water sloshed over the side of the bath.

In his entire life he knew he would never forget the sight of the woman he loved bringing herself to climax in front of her two lovers. The image was burned in his brain for eternity.

Chapter Two

Slow down, she chanted to herself. Breathe deep. Put one foot in front of the other. That's it. Good. Now walk. Just keep walking.

The glass doors loomed ahead of her.

She was doing fine. Her next task: pull the handle and walk outside. Then get as far away from him as possible.

The cool air of the autumn morning washed across her face, and she sucked in the fresh air, clutching the sketch pad like a lifeline. Better. Maybe she'd be able to think straight now. Sort out her boggled brain. Impossible accomplishment with Gabriel Carter sitting opposite her. Impossible.

God. *Gabe.* What was he doing there? She clenched her fist at her side to stop her hand from trembling.

Tina collapsed against the back of the bath, shivers of delight still washing over her. Lord, the effect these two men had on her. Just their presence turned her on. She hadn't meant to touch herself in front of them. But what choice did she have? Connor lounged against the shower door, looking for all the world like a movie star, and Gabe was perched on the side of the bath, his sexual prowess sending tentacles of desire snaking through her loins.

And so casual about it all too. Dropping by to say hello as if nothing had ever gone wrong between them. As if he hadn't walked out of her life without a second glance. Damn it. Why did it still have to hurt? Why did the memories still burn the back of her throat?

"Tina. Wait!"

She kept walking. Fast. Heading anywhere that wasn't near Gabe.

She might as well not have bothered. Less than ten paces down the path he caught up with her. A hand on her shoulder halted any further progress. Not that the hand demanded in any way. Quite the opposite. It was so gentle, she almost couldn't feel it. However, the energy snapping between her flesh and his palm was impossible to ignore.

Tina bit back a groan. Lord, how did he do that? Send heat flowing through her with nothing more than the lightest touch.

Before the last tremors of pleasure fluttered through her, Gabe leaned over and plucked her from the bath. Water streamed from her body, drenching him. He seemed not to notice. He tucked her on his lap, with her ass planted on the seat of his huge, muscular thighs, tilted her head and slanted his mouth over hers.

Her orgasm had left her lazy and sated, but his lips awakened a new fire. Flames flared, burning away any trace of satisfaction. She wiggled on his lap, desperate to feel his rigid erection pushing against her butt.

"Tina, please. Don't leave. Not yet." His voice was low, not quite a whisper behind her ear.

She couldn't do this, couldn't be with him. Even now, years later, the pain of his sudden retreat stung. Tina had been happiest when she was with him and Connor. She had been fulfilled and satisfied and content. With no warning, Gabe had left. He'd just walked away, ripping her heart out as he went. Connor had followed soon after. Not that she hadn't expected it.

23

Without Gabe, the magic had dissipated. Without Gabe, she and Connor did not work. The enchantment of their relationship was gone.

She couldn't face him. "I didn't leave, Gabe. You did."

There was nothing behind her to fill the aching emptiness in her chest her words had created, nothing but silence. Dead silence. Then a shuffle. His hand moved down to her arm. The warmth from his palm seeped through her shirt, through her flesh and into her bones.

Regret laced his tone. "I hurt you, didn't I?"

He tasted liked heaven. Like man and sex all rolled into one. His tongue stroked hers, his arms caressed her sides, her back. His immense chest crushed her breasts, sending intoxicating tingles rushing through the sensitive tips.

It wasn't enough. When it came to Gabe and Connor she always wanted more.

He stepped closer behind her, placed his other hand on her other arm, and shockwaves pulsed through her torso. "If it makes you feel better, I hurt me too."

"Why on earth do you think that would make me feel better?"

He made a funny sound, as though he were being strangled. "I'm not thinking much of anything now, T, other than how good it is to see you. I just want to say hello. It's been a long time."

Whose fault was that? If things had panned out the way she wished they would have, he could have seen her every day—and night—for the last forty-eight or so months. "This isn't a good idea, Gabe. We've said hello. I need to go."

"Go where? To your...man?"

What did he know about *her man*? She whipped round and

found herself staring daggers at Gabe's chest. God, he was enormous. A veritable mountain of a man.

Gabe released her just long enough for Tina to turn and then his hands were back, gently gripping her. "I saw him kiss you goodbye." He shrugged. "I put two and two together. Well, one and one together." He said it with a marked casualness, but the narrowing of his eyes belied his tone. He was more than a little bothered by what he'd seen.

Too bad. His problems weren't hers, and she sure as hell did not feel like him sharing them with her right now. Instead she answered with a twist of sarcasm. "And I always thought you were better at putting two and one together."

Gabe released her mouth and spun her round, curving his powerful chest against her wet back and offering her a view of Connor's impressive erection. He cupped her breasts with his huge hands, ran his thumbs over her nipples, and she moaned.

Connor opened a drawer, took out two condoms and pushed the drawer closed.

Moisture dripped between her legs. "Just one for now," she said, her voice husky even to her own ears. "It's all we're going to need."

Gabe growled behind her.

His grip tightened, not painfully, but enough so his fingers molded to her flesh. He stared down at her mouth. She glared up into his eyes. There was nothing casual about the way he looked at her. His eyes were black, disturbed. Was he imagining Anthony with her? Was that a flash of anger in his dark gaze?

And then he blinked and released her, smoothing the material on her shirt where he'd gripped her arms.

"Does he make you happy, T?" he asked.

She gaped up at him. What kind of a question was that?

"That is none of your business."

"You looked sad after he left. It worried me. I want to make sure you're happy."

"Just like you were so intent on ensuring my happiness when you walked out on me? On us?"

She'd gotten a taste of Gabe; now she wanted more. She wanted to taste him intimately, deeply. She wanted to pull him as far into her mouth as she could take him. Just like she wanted Connor as deep in her body as he could get.

"Put the condom on, C," she told Connor as she pushed off Gabe's lap, twisted round to face him and knelt between his legs. "Put it on and get over here."

Gabe lifted his arms in surrender. Arms that were thick and muscled. No wonder she'd loved burrowing into his embrace so much. She'd curl up against his chest and feel cherished, protected and safe. She'd never felt as safe as when Gabe held her.

"Guilty as charged. I walked out on you." Something flickered in his eyes. Pain? "God knows it was the hardest thing I've ever done."

"Is that supposed to be an apology?" She gaped at him. "That's real slick, Gabe. Let's stand in the middle of the footpath, with people walking all around us, and you apologize for breaking my heart four years ago. That'll make everything right between us."

A muscle worked in his cheek. "I don't want to stand here. I want to sit somewhere, quiet, just the two of us and...talk."

Gabe's erection sprung proud from his lap, thick and enticing. Her mouth watered as she placed her lips on the tip and indulged in the tiniest lick.

He groaned above her and wrapped his fingers in her hair.

26

She swirled her tongue around the head of his cock.

"Christ, that's a turn-on," Connor said behind her, his voice rough as sandpaper.

Need echoed through her belly. She pushed her butt out, inviting Connor closer without releasing Gabe. There was very little she relished more in this world than having her two men together at the same time.

She smiled around Gabe's dick.

She sighed. "I don't want to talk."

"Fine. I'll talk, you listen."

She shot him a dubious look. Gabe Carter didn't talk.

He smiled then. A small, teasing smile that lifted the corners of his mouth in a manner so delightful and sexy it took her breath away. "Try me. Give me half an hour. You won't have to say one thing in all that time. Not one word. I will take on sole responsibility for any conversation."

She shook her head. God, she wanted to give him a chance, wanted desperately to hear what he had to say, but he'd broken her heart once. She could not, would not, give him another opportunity. "I'm not interested, Gabe."

"Thirty minutes. That's it. After that you can walk away." His gaze held hers, fire burning behind their dark façade. "If you still want to."

Connor knelt behind her. His hands brushed over the bare flesh of her back, his erection nestled between her buttocks.

She whimpered and pressed back against him. Her lower lips swelled. It didn't matter that mere minutes had passed since her orgasm. She hungered for more, hungered for the relief Connor could provide with the slightest thrust of his hips.

Holding herself steady with one hand on Gabe's leg, she wrapped the other around his shaft and licked him from the base of his penis all the way to the top. Gabe rewarded her with a few precious beads of pre-come and a throaty growl.

"What are you going to say, Gabe? What can you tell me in half an hour that'll make me want to stay longer? You're wasting your breath."

"Aren't you the least bit inquisitive? What if I tell you something that'll change your life? Or maybe you'll find out something that changed mine. The one thing I can promise for sure is if you don't give me the chance you'll never know."

Damn him. He'd always known how to pique her interest. More often than not he'd done it with his body or with a whispered promise of passion, but every once in a while he'd say something that would have her lifting her chin in curiosity.

"How do you want it, T?" Connor pulled back, and then he was there again, dragging the tip of his cock through her slick folds, mercilessly teasing her.

"Here?" He dipped an inch inside her, making her gasp. "Or here?" He trailed a path away from her pussy and up through the cleft of her buttocks. Then, light as a feather, he touched his dick to the sensitive bud of her ass.

Decidedly lightheaded, Tina began to shake. "Either... Both. Doesn't...matter." It didn't make a difference. She just wanted Connor inside her. As much as she wanted Gabe.

Connor drew his dick down to her pussy again, torturing her aching flesh. He dipped inside, delighting her, only to pull away again and repeat the journey upwards.

No! Not enough. She wanted him inside.

She licked the soft skin around Gabe's testicles. If Connor could taunt her with unfulfilled promises, she'd taunt Gabe in the same way. Fair was fair.

"Christ, Regan," Gabe bit out. "Stop teasing her. I can't take

it."

Tina narrowed her eyes in anger. "You had your chance to change my life. You chose not to take it." Aw, crap. Why did she have to keep harping on this? Why couldn't she just let bygones be bygones? The last thing she needed was for Gabe to discover he'd hurt her so profoundly.

"I was a fool." There it was again, that look in his eyes, the one that resembled pain. He stepped back, moving out of her personal space. "I'm sorry. You obviously don't want to talk to me. I won't waste your time anymore."

Relief flooded through her. Now she could get away from Gabe, escape the enchanting spell he cast over her with such ease. "Thank you." She gave a short nod. "See you around." *Or not.*

Shit, it didn't make sense. Escape was imminent. So how did she explain the waves of disappointment?

The bathroom echoed with Connor's chuckle. "Where do you want it, T?" he asked again as he nudged into her pussy once more.

She didn't give him a chance to pull away this time. With a quick, sharp twist, she pushed back on him, impaling herself on his cock.

Connor's laughter turned to a gruff moan.

God, he felt good. Long and satisfying, he more than filled her. But one man wasn't enough. Not with Gabe there as well. Widening her legs to give Connor better access, she brought her mouth to the tip of Gabe's cock and, inch by inch, took him in as far as he would go.

"T," Gabe gasped. "Damn...that's...just... Damn."

Tina walked away. Again she put one foot in front of the other, willing herself to go. Four years, she told herself. No way should she feel this cut-up after four years. Go. Just go.

"Did you know that you changed my life?" he called after her.

She stopped dead in her tracks.

"After you I was never the same."

She swiveled around slowly.

"You changed me. You changed who I was."

Her willpower and determination evaporated.

Tina mimicked Connor's every move. As he pulled back, she pulled back, leaving just the tip of Gabe's dick in her mouth. When Connor thrust forward, so did she, swallowing as much of Gabe as she was able. When Connor moved slowly and sensually, tantalizing her inner walls, she sucked slowly and sensually, savoring the taste and the fullness of Gabe against her tongue. God, she loved giving Gabe blowjobs. Loved his uneven panting and incoherent mutterings. Loved how this enormous bear of a man came apart in her mouth. Loved that with all his massive bulk and hard muscle he was the most tender, gentlest lover she'd ever known.

As Connor increased the pace, so did she. The nerves in her pussy screamed for release, begging for the satisfaction she knew was moments away. Connor's expertise had her hanging on a string. Sensation built. Desire rose. Soon, very soon. She was so close.

She increased her attention to Gabe, loving him wholly and completely with her mouth, using her hand to pump the parts of his cock her mouth could not reach. Connor's thrusts became harder, more focused. His hand crept around her waist, delved into her curls and found her clit.

Gabe stiffened. His balls constricted.

Connor drove into her, hard and fast. His finger circled her nub.

The world around her narrowed and faded. Sensation spiked, causing violent tremors to wrack her body. Gabe exploded in her mouth. She clasped her lips around him, conscious of nothing besides the need to swallow every last drop and the intense, mind-blowing pleasure Connor wrenched out of her.

Her inner muscles clenched repeatedly around Connor, who gave one mighty, final thrust and erupted.

Tina collapsed on Gabe's lap. Waves of satisfaction still pulsed through her body. But that was not her overwhelming sense. Right here, right now, with Gabe and Connor, she was happy. Complete. With these two men she was whole.

"You have half an hour, Gabe. Make it count."

Chapter Three

Now what?

Stare at her like a complete moron, unable to believe she'd just agreed to give him his requested thirty minutes? Or make the time count?

Tina stood before him, her sketch pad clutched beneath one trembling arm. At least he wasn't the only one feeling all shaky and unhinged.

The cover of the pad was missing, allowing him glimpses of a pencil stroke-filled page. Gabe knew whatever the full picture was, it would be filled with detail and drenched with emotion.

And that was when the epiphany struck.

Taking two giant strides towards her, he enfolded her free hand in his and propelled her forward. "Come with me, T."

Sure, he'd used the cheesy "life-changing" line to snare her attention, but now he intended to see it through. He'd disappointed Tina enough already. This time he would not.

"Where are you taking me?" she panted, struggling to keep up with him.

Gabe adjusted his gait, slowing down to suit Tina's shorter legs. Standing a little over five feet, there was no way she could maintain his pace. Her small hand burned holes in his bigger one, the warmth of her skin and the daintiness of her fingers reminding him of a touch he had never forgotten. "To a friend's place."

Tina planted her feet on the ground and refused to take another step. For a woman with such a small frame she had a surprising amount of strength. "You mean to Connor's place," she accused.

"Connor?" Gabe asked, confused. And then understanding dawned. He shook his head in disbelief. "You think I'm taking you there so we can pick up where we left off? Seduce you all over again?"

She shrugged. "Aren't you?"

"You jump to conclusions." Of course he wasn't taking her back to Connor's place. Gabe refused to contemplate the possibility of sharing Tina again. If he ever won her back—and that might be hard considering the man in the coffee shop— he would have her to himself. Period.

Tina sniffed and took a tentative step forward. "So, where are you taking me?"

Gabe pursed his lips in thought and then answered carefully. "You changed my life. I thought I might return the favor."

"Shit, Gabe. I am not going to sleep with you."

Even if I beg? "I'm not talking about sex."

This time she had the decency to look abashed. "Sorry," she mumbled. "I guess it's difficult not to associate sex with you and Connor."

"S'okay," he mumbled back. "I make the same associations with you." Only the associations didn't stop at sex. They incorporated his blood heating to boiling point, his throat burning with unspoken admissions and his heart aching with loneliness.

He tugged her hand, propelling them both back into walk mode. Then he flashed her a wicked smile. "But I'm honored to hear you equate sex with me with a life-changing event."

Tina opened her mouth to answer then snapped it shut.

"Speechless?" Gabe laughed out loud. "There's a first. Usually I'm the one left without a thing to say." His body was in all sorts of hell. Walking beside Tina, with her shoulder brushing his arm, her hand in his and her hip swaying against his thigh, was nothing less than agony. Four years ago, he wouldn't have minded. Four years ago, he'd have pulled her to a stop, turned to face her and taken her lips in a bone-melting kiss. He'd have molded her body to his and ground his erection against her belly, leaving her with no doubt as to the effect she had on his libido.

Tina glanced at her watch. "Twenty-seven minutes left. Better make the most of them."

Gabe ushered her across the road to his car. "Jump in." He opened the door for her. "And take that look off your face. I'm not kidnapping you. After my half hour is up I promise to drop you right back here." He hesitated a heartbeat before adding, "If you still want me to."

Without waiting for her response, he whipped round to the driver's seat and set off in the direction of his friend's house. Tina's scent—her exotic, alluring perfume—wafted through his nose and settled in his stomach like hunger. Each soft breath she took reverberated in his ears and echoed through his chest.

A lot could happen in four years, Gabe acknowledged. Time tended to change a person, shaping them through new experiences. This Tina could be very different from his precious T. But if she was, his body seemed not to have noticed. He still reacted to her on base instinct. His stomach still lurched when he looked at her, and his groin still tightened when she looked at him.

He wanted to ask again what had made her so sad, but as he'd promised to take all responsibility of making conversation away from her, he chose not to. Instead he searched his brain for some neutral topic of conversation—and came up blank.

Tina saved him. "How *is* Connor?" she asked as Gabe contemplated a tight curve in the road.

"He's okay. Quite good really. He met a woman."

"He did?"

"Yep. Fell pretty hard for her."

"Nice woman?"

"Very," Gabe said.

Something about his answer must have given him away. "Was she one of *your* women?"

Gabe frowned. "You ask that as though we've had so many."

She straightened her shoulders. "I don't know how many you've had, and frankly, I don't care. But you have that gleam on your face, leaving me to assume you and Connor shared her. Just the way you shared me."

She was right. They had shared her. But that was where the similarity ended. Gabe had never fallen in love with Maddie, and Connor had never been in love with Tina. "Yes," he said. "She was our lover."

Tina pursed her lips. "So, Connor went ahead and introduced you to a woman he loved?"

"Not quite. I, er, met her first." About a month ago. "I introduced Connor to Maddie."

"Interesting," Tina murmured under her breath.

"What is?"

"That Connor fell for her. What happened to your understanding? How does it go? Only the man who meets the woman first gets to fall in love with her?"

Gabe overstepped the brake, and the car ground to a sudden halt. "How do you know about that?"

Tina would not look him in the eye. "How do you think I know? Connor told me."

"When?" Gabe rasped. Christ, she knew about his and Connor's pact.

She stared out of her window. "Before he introduced me to you. Before anything happened. I was...uh...nervous. He reassured me. Told me you had strict rules that you play by."

Gabe cleared his throat. "We abandoned the rules. They weren't working." He eased his foot back onto the accelerator.

"When?"

"This morning." He wished it had been four years ago. Wished he'd had the guts to do for himself then what he'd done for Connor now. But rules were rules, and he'd stuck to them. Put his friendship with Connor before his love for a woman. Just like Connor had been willing to do for him today.

About bloody time one of them came to their senses.

"So, Connor's off the market." she said with a marked casualness.

Gabe listened for any other undertones to her statement. Anything that might resemble regret or disappointment. Anything that might suggest she'd had feelings for Connor. "Looks that way."

"Lucky girl," Tina whispered.

"Lucky Connor," Gabe countered. Connor had found what he'd been looking for. Someone to fill up the emptiness in his life. A very nice someone at that.

Tina turned sharply to look at him. "Are you okay? About Connor falling for your girlfriend, I mean?"

Gabe's answering smile was genuine. "Sure I am. They're good for each other. They'll be good together." If he hadn't believed that, he'd never have insisted Connor and Maddie stay together—just the two of them.

He made a left, then a right and pulled up outside a house.

Tina checked her watch. "Nineteen minutes," she warned, and he suppressed the urge to kiss her senseless.

"Then let's not waste time." He had less than twenty minutes to convince Tina to let him back into her life. Twenty minutes within which his future happiness rested. Well, at least a shot at his future happiness. He climbed out of his car.

Tina followed suit.

"Uh uh," Gabe warned. "Don't leave your sketch pad behind. Bring it along." If he was going to change her life he needed the pad. And damn, he wanted to make a difference to her future. Almost as much as he wanted to be a part of it.

Tina shrugged and did as he said. They walked up the pathway of a small, picturesque house with a beautiful landscaped garden. Several strategically placed sculptures highlighted a water feature and a rock garden. It was a yard worthy of a feature in *Better Homes and Gardens.*

"Okay, I'm curious. Where are we?" Tina asked as she looked around.

"Ever heard of Valerie Carnell?" He kept his gaze on her. As beautiful as the garden was, it paled in comparison to her.

Tina sighed. "Don't tell me. She's another one of your women."

Gabe laughed out loud. "Not even close. We met a while back, at a fundraiser organized by the children's cancer ward at the hospital." Gabe had had a special interest in the fundraiser since he'd treated several patients from the ward in his physical therapy practice.

Tina nodded. "I heard about that. It was a photographic exhibition right?"

Gabe nodded and rang the front doorbell. "Right. I got to know Valerie then. She's an amazing woman. I think you'll like her."

Tina wrinkled her nose, an action Gabe had always found both sexy and endearing. This time wasn't any different, he realized, as his ribs tightened around his heart. "I don't understand. Why are you bringing me to meet her?"

"Because, T, she can help you."

The front door swung open, revealing a middle-aged woman brightly clad in an ankle-length dress comprised of layer upon layer of colorful silk. At least Gabe assumed it was silk. His knowledge of dress fabric was, he supposed, limited at best.

Her face lit up at the sight of him. "Gabriel!" She threw her arms open, and he stepped into her welcoming hug. "Darling. To what do I owe the pleasure?" She pulled back and gave him both of her cheeks to kiss.

"Val—" he smiled, "—I've brought someone to meet you. Someone I think you'll like. A lot." He angled his body so Valerie could see Tina. "Tina Jenkins."

Valerie appraised her with obvious interest. Then she returned her gaze to Gabe and lifted a speculative eyebrow.

Gabe resisted the urge to shift beneath her scrutiny.

"Why Gabriel, she's just a little bit of a thing. Doesn't even reach your shoulders. I couldn't see her standing behind you." She stuck out her arm and took Tina's hand in hers. "A pleasure to meet you, my dear."

Tina looked at her with big eyes. "Uh, and you too."

"Is that a sketch pad I spy?" Valerie asked, staring at Tina's other arm.

Tina tensed, as if drawing the pad closer to her body. "It is," she answered hesitantly.

Valerie smiled up at Gabe. "Well, then. Why don't you two come right on inside and we can chat." She turned around and bustled them both through the door.

Tina shot Gabe an inquiring look. She held one palm up as if to say, "Who is she?"

Gabe grinned. "You know the gallery where the exhibition took place?" He winked at her. "Valerie owns it."

Tina wanted to skip down the path towards Gabe's car. She couldn't remember the last time she'd felt like skipping, the last time she'd been this excited about anything.

"Don't pinch me," she warned Gabe. "If this is a dream I do not want to wake up."

"It's not a dream." His grin was infectious. She couldn't help but smile back. "Val loved your work."

"My own exhibition? Can you believe it?" She threw her head back and laughed. "She wants to show my sketches. Wants to *sell* them. Who would have thought it?"

Gabe's hand on her arm stopped her in her tracks. "I would have." The look on his face whipped the air from her lungs. He stared at her with hooded, hungry eyes. "Anyone who's ever seen them would believe it." The mixture of lust and respect in his expression almost brought her to her knees.

Except she'd been on her knees with Gabe before. She'd worshipped him on her knees, pleasured him, taken him to the same incredible heights he'd taken her—and still he'd left her. It didn't matter how he looked at her now or how much her own body ached to respond to the desire burning in his gaze, she would not give in to her impulses. No matter how grateful she was to him for introducing her to Valerie.

She swung away from him, feigning a playfulness she no longer felt. "How am I ever going to lug all my sketch pads to her gallery? I must have one hundred of them."

"It's not a problem. I'll help you," Gabe offered. "Unless..." The fire in his eyes dimmed and he shrugged. "It's been a lot longer than thirty minutes."

Tina checked her watch, stunned to see over two hours had passed since they'd arrived at Valerie's. And just like that her heart dipped in her chest. Gabe's half hour was up, long ago.

Thank God for that. Now she could walk away and not look back. What a relief.

He opened the car door for her. "Would you like me to drop you back at the coffee shop?"

Tina stared at him. That would be the best idea. The car trip would give her ample time to thank him for introducing her to Valerie, and then she could get away from him. Perhaps she'd send him a gift tomorrow. A bottle of wine. Or scotch. Something to express her gratitude. At least she wouldn't be trapped beside him any longer, yearning to pick up where they'd left off four years ago. Yearning to feel his and Connor's hands on her body again, their lips on her mouth.

"I could drop you at home?"

Nope, bad idea. She'd feel compelled to invite him in.

"Or I could do what I've been wanting to for the last few hours and take you in my arms and kiss you."

Tina's jaw fell open. "What—?"

Gabe's gaze dropped to her mouth. He shook his head. "Not just the last few hours," he said hoarsely. "The last four years."

Her vocal powers eluded her. There was not one single thing she could think of to say in response. Not one.

"Christ, T, I've dreamed of seeing you again." His massive hand was on her cheek now, and he dragged his thumb over her lower lip. "Kissing you again."

A wave of dizziness washed over her. Never mind the powers of speech, she couldn't think straight.

"Dreamed of touching you." His thumb traced the curve of her upper lip. "Tasting you."

Her breath caught in her throat.

"I've dreamed of you. Every night for four years." Even as he said it he bent forward. She watched, spellbound, as he closed the distance between them. With a soft groan, he pressed his mouth to hers.

She turned to mush. Standing on the footpath beside his car, with his lips on hers, she couldn't breathe. She couldn't think or talk. She could hardly hold herself upright. Her bones dissolved in her legs and her arms lost all structure. Gabe's lips were on hers—warm, soft and seductive. Gabe. Oh, dear Lord, Gabe.

He drew back to stare into her eyes. "Christ..." he whispered. "I've wanted you for four years." And then his mouth was on hers again, his tongue slipping between her lips, and she melted into him.

God help her, she hadn't meant to respond, but how could she resist the temptation that was Gabe Carter?

Sensing her capitulation, his arms closed around her, pulling her in even closer, and she lost herself in his immense size, in his taste, in his familiar, spicy scent. Had anyone ever made her feel the way Gabe and Connor did?

All it had taken with them was one kiss, and she was reduced to a trembling wreck. Nothing had changed. Shivers raced through her as Gabe deepened the kiss, reminding her how each cell in her body had always responded to the two men, how every nerve fiber had stood to attention when they touched her.

He lifted her up, curving her body into his. His chest was a solid mass against her breasts, his legs thick and muscled against her thighs. In this position it was impossible to ignore the girth of his erection straining against her belly. Its very presence made her weak-kneed and lightheaded. It also made her horny. Very, very horny.

His tongue danced with hers. His taste filled her mouth. Sex and man.

No one had tasted quite so enticing as Gabe or Connor.

And no one had hurt her quite as profoundly as Gabe.

The thought knocked a little sense into her, giving her the strength to pull away. His arms might have been firm as steel rings around her waist, but the second she struggled against them they relaxed, allowing her to step down. Yet again, Tina was reminded of just how safe she'd always felt with him. No matter his size or his strength, he would never use it against her.

Just like that she was free. Released from the all-consuming embrace that fogged her mind and clouded her body with desire. Her breasts were heavy within the tight constraints of her bra, and her chest heaved in a futile attempt to draw breath.

No one had hurt her quite as profoundly as Gabe.

"You can take me home, thank you." She stepped back, squared her shoulders and glared at him. Then wished she hadn't. Glaring at Gabe meant staring him straight in the face. And what a face. His lips, full and succulent at the most platonic of times, were now swollen from their kiss. His eyes were dark and even more hooded than before. Desire seeped from beneath his heavy lids.

Christ, he looked edible. More than edible, he looked downright fuckable. If she didn't wrap her head around the fact that this was the very man who had stomped all over her heart and her trust, she would jump him. Right here, outside the house of the woman who had just offered her the chance of a lifetime.

"Ah, T, there is nothing I would like more than to take you home." His words were draped in velvet and served to her with a light sprinkling of breathlessness and a thick promise of sex. "Take you home, strip you of your clothes and your inhibitions and make love to you for the rest of the day." He swallowed. "The rest of the week."

Shit. She was gawking again. Staring all bug-eyed at him. And why couldn't she hold her darn mouth shut? Why'd her jaw have to hang open like some speechless moron who couldn't put a sentence together? And please, someone—anyone—tell her she wasn't drooling. Please.

"Take me home and leave me there," she corrected in a cold voice, embracing her inner bitch. "You're right. Your thirty minutes is long over."

Gabe drew back as though she'd slapped him.

For an instant she regretted her unkind words. But just for an instant. "You were true to your word. You did change my life today. And I thank you for that. But..." She bit her lip. "But you're four years too late, and my sketches were never the part of my life that needed changing." Her vision blurred, and she had to feign an interest in her sketch pad. She'd be damned if she'd let Gabe know he was still worthy of her tears.

A minute passed, then another. The silence stretched out, fraught with unspoken memories. Neither of them moved.

As though it was the last thing in the world he wanted to do, Gabe nodded. He stepped away from her and opened the passenger door of his car. Tina climbed in.

"Are you still in the same flat?" he asked in a stilted voice once he was in the driver's seat.

She nodded. Four years and very little had changed. Her address was still the same. Her life was still the same, her feelings for Gabe and Connor were still the same, and the hurt cut just as deeply as it always had.

The five-minute car ride home seemed to stretch into five hours. Several times Gabe opened his mouth as if to speak, and several times he closed it again without saying a word. His hands clenched the steering wheel, the skin over his fists stretched taut and white. Muscles bulged in his arms as he flexed his biceps over and over.

Tina turned her attention to the road and pretended not to notice. She would not weaken her resolve. It didn't matter how strong the physical attraction still was between her and Gabe, or how much she wanted to invite him home for the week. She would not make herself vulnerable to him again.

"Thank you," she said formally when he pulled up outside her unit. "Introducing me to Valerie was...thoughtful of you." She kept her voice restrained. Her earlier excitement about meeting Val had gotten her into trouble. The hot, sensual kind of trouble of which she did not need more. "Would...would you be interested in coming to the exhibition?" How could she not invite him? Without him there wouldn't even be a show. "Perhaps you could bring Connor along. And Maggie."

"Maddie," Gabe corrected, his voice even quieter than it had been earlier. He shrugged. "Perhaps. Send me an invitation?"

Tina gave a short, sharp nod and snapped open her seatbelt.

"I'm sorry, T," Gabe said before she moved. "I never meant to hurt you, ever."

She couldn't deal with the tone she heard in his voice. Was it anger? Frustration? Pain? She didn't want to think about it, didn't want to give Gabe any more of her time. It would only crack open her heart further and let him creep inside all over again. She had to get away from him.

"Look, no worries," she said with a casualness she did not feel. "What was, was. Let's just leave it in the past, shall we?" She braved a glance in his direction and immediately wished she hadn't.

Gabe looked at her with much the same expression he'd worn when they'd made love—alone—for the first time. Connor had been away for the weekend, and he'd given them his blessing to "have fun".

Gabe's brown eyes had burned with a molten fire when he'd laid her down on the carpet and kissed her until her logic receded to the furthest recesses of her mind, and all she could contemplate was Gabe. He'd kissed her until she writhed beneath him, begging for more, and then he'd undressed her, removing each item of clothing with exquisite tenderness. He'd made love to her that day. That day she'd *felt* loved by him— and it was the first time she'd realized she loved him. Him and Connor.

And just look where that dumb emotion had gotten her.

Tina came tumbling back to the present with a resounding crash. She shoved the door open and scrambled out the car. It was time to shove Gabe and her memories back into the past.

"Thank you again. I'll be sure to get the invitation out to you." Then she closed the door behind her, turned and walked away.

Chapter Four

Gabe tore away from the footpath, tires screeching. The needle of the speedometer hit over eighty kilometers per hour in less than a minute.

Fuck!

Checking his rearview mirror long enough to ensure there was no one behind him, he veered to the side of the road, slammed on his brakes and stalled the car.

Good fucking thing too, because in this mood he might kill some unsuspecting pedestrian—or himself, overstepping the curves at Bronte and sending the car careening through the barriers and over the sheer rock face of the cliffs into the raging ocean below.

Fuck. Fuck, fuck, fuck.

That had gone about as well as a baby 'roo thrown to a pack of starving dingoes. She'd chewed him up and spat him out. He grimaced. At least she hadn't spat *at* him. If the look on her face as she climbed out the car had been anything to go by, that was sheer luck on his part.

God, she must despise him. Think him the biggest shit on earth. He'd known he'd hurt when he left her. He hadn't guessed at how much he'd hurt her. Christ, he'd just wanted to do the right thing. By her and by Connor. She was Connor's. He'd met her first. He'd told Gabe how much he dug her. No.

Connor had never loved her, nor had he intimated that he loved her. But rules were rules. It was either sacrifice a lifetime of friendship with Connor and express his true feelings to Tina, or give up Tina and protect all three of them in the process.

When rules got broken, people got hurt. Connor was his best mate, and Tina was the woman he loved. No way he'd hurt either of them. Easier to just pull away and leave Connor and Tina alone to be happy together. Let him be the only one to experience the pain.

Only that wasn't how it had played out. His abrupt departure *had* hurt Tina. Badly. Badly enough that she wanted nothing to do with him anymore. Yes, she was grateful for the introduction to Valerie today, but that was where it ended. She didn't want anything else from him.

She had a boyfriend now, just like she'd had one three and a half years ago when he'd gone in search of her the first time. The man in the coffee shop was one lucky fuck. Sharp blades of jealousy cut at Gabe's gut. Was it the same guy? Had they been together all this time?

Gabe rubbed his hand over his face, contempt for himself and for Tina's man souring his mouth. Which was a damn pity, because the last thing he'd tasted was Tina's sweet breath. Her hot tongue. Just thinking about the kiss they'd shared outside Valerie's house made him hard all over again. The way she'd collapsed against him, her curves branding his muscles.

Gabe froze.

She'd kissed him back. Opened her soft lips and given as much as she'd taken. She'd fused her mouth to his and kissed him with all the passion and heat of four years ago. Yes, she'd pulled away, come to her senses. That didn't change the fact that she'd kissed him back.

Gabe threw the car into neutral and turned the key. He'd

loved the woman for over four years. He'd finally allowed himself the pleasure of talking to her again, of kissing her again—and she'd kissed him back. No matter how much she might despise him, there was still something somewhere inside her that responded to him. And damned if he wasn't going to explore it further.

Tina slumped when the doorbell rang. Not company. Not now. Please. Her day had gone from bad to worse to unbelievable to nerve-wracking to heartbreaking all in one morning. She had no strength to make small talk with visitors.

One failed relationship in the morning, followed by a surprise visit from an old lover, topped off by an offer of an exhibition was enough excitement to push any woman over the edge.

She put her pad and granite stick aside and stood reluctantly. With a bit of luck it would be someone spreading the word of God, and she could make some polite excuse and get this over and done with. She opened the door.

"Do you love him?"

Shit.

"Do you?"

Her heart performed a series of erratic somersaults. "Love who?"

"The guy I saw you with earlier. The one who kissed you in the coffee bar."

Anthony? "I told you already. It's none of your business."

"You kissed him, T. For a long time."

He filled the doorway. His shoulders seemed to reach from one side of the doorjamb to the other. God, how she'd loved running her hands over those shoulders. Loved the feel of his muscles tensing beneath her touch. "You kissed me, Gabe. For a long time. Does it mean you love me?"

His upper lip twisted. "I'll answer that question later. I just want to know if you love him."

"Why? What difference does it make?"

"It makes a shitload of difference. If you don't love him, I won't regret doing this."

"Doing wh—?"

Her question was cut off mid-word. Gabe swooped forward and caught her mouth in a fierce kiss. He gave her not a second to object. She was aware of three things. The slamming of a door, a sense of weightlessness as he hauled her off the ground and held her in a tight, all-encompassing embrace, and the sheer glory of his tongue sweeping past her lips.

God, he tasted good. Like the long-forgotten sugar of a childhood treat. Now that she'd sampled it again she wanted more. More, more, more.

Instinct took over. She wound her legs around his waist and kissed him back, licking into his mouth, desperate to devour every last ounce of sweetness. Her nipples tightened as they pressed against the solidness of his chest, and she wrapped her arms around his neck.

Her groin clenched as her clit ground against him, making her whimper.

He wrenched his lips from hers. "Say it," he rasped. "Tell me you don't love him."

She was incapable of speech. All she wanted was the heat of his mouth back on hers. She sought his lips blindly, found them and locked her mouth to his. His hands were on her ass, molded to her cheeks. The heat from his palms scorched her straight through her jeans. He kneaded her butt, pulling her cheeks apart as far as they'd go within the confines of the denim and then pushing them back together so the string of her thong scraped against her skin. As he kneaded he pushed harder against her, massaging her intimately.

Again he pulled back from her kiss. "Damn it. Tell me you don't love him." His eyes were scrunched closed.

She nipped his jaw.

"S-say it." He dipped her lower, introducing her clit to his rock-hard erection, rubbing her against it until she yelped and heat flooded her pussy.

Shit, she could climax just like this.

"W-want to make you come, T." He thrust his groin against hers, over and over, sending flaming darts of pleasure shooting straight into her. "Want you to explode in my arms. Just tell me you don't love the fucker. Please."

"Don't...don't love...him." She ground down hard against his cock, her clit a mass of sensitive nerve endings. "Ended things...this...oh, God...morning."

His growl of satisfaction echoed through her ears, and he bucked wildly against her. "Now," he ordered as his denim-encased cock seemed to grow against her. "Come..." he continued his frenzied thrusting, driving her insane beyond comprehension, "...now."

She fragmented in his arms, a million pleasure points pulsing through her pussy. Tremors wracked her body as the release tore through her.

"One." Gabe's voice echoed through her ears. He walked her backwards and leaned over. Her back touched something soft, and just like that she was sprawled on her couch with Gabe kneeling on the floor before her.

"At least another three," he told her and stripped off her jeans. Her sodden thong followed seconds later.

God, Gabe was counting. Which meant he wasn't done making her come. Not by a long shot. Dimly she told herself to get up. To show a little backbone. But her breathing hadn't yet regulated, and her legs were paralyzed. She couldn't move now even if she wanted to.

"Gabe!" She groaned as he leaned over her and buried his face between her legs. His tongue was hot and wet against her, soothing. Jeans were not the softest of material, and mashing her pussy against her pants and his, while most erotic, left her requiring just a bit of recovery time. Or better yet—treatment. Warm, moist treatment, that took away the tenderness and replaced it once again with blazing lust. He licked her with a gentleness that touched her heart, and he licked her with a possessiveness that tingled down her spine. Then he licked her with a lust that jarred through her belly and sent shudders shivering through her.

His tongue seduced and teased. It laved and calmed while it caressed and excited. It drove her halfway to heaven, then withdrew, leaving her hanging on the precipice, desperate for release.

"Come for me, Tina," he said, his breath teasing the lips of her pussy. "Now." He licked her again, and she dissolved around his tongue, tremors of ecstasy flowing through her.

He gave her no recovery time. As the waves of her orgasm shuddered through her, he dipped two fingers inside her. Her inner walls reacted on instinct, clamping down around them. Christ, it shouldn't feel so familiar after four years. So right. But it did. So right, her body tumbled into a fresh set of tremors.

Her head was a jumble of confusion. Chaos reigned

supreme. She couldn't think straight, couldn't remember why it was so important she keep her distance from Gabe. Why on earth would she want to stay away from a man who could bring her to climax three times in minutes? What had he done that was so bad?

She knew he'd done something, knew it was serious enough that the pain had not subsided for a very long time, but details eluded her. Most everything escaped her now, apart from the play of his tongue against her pussy lips.

He turned her, seating her upright so she leaned against the back of the couch. He spread her legs and propped her feet up on his shoulders, exposing her core completely to his invading tongue. He made love to her with his mouth, adored her, played symphonies on her inner lips. And then he cupped his hands beneath her ass and lifted her hips higher, dragging his tongue just a couple of millimeters lower. He tickled the crevice between her butt cheeks before dipping in to taste her ass.

The breath left her body in a loud sigh. God knew Gabe was gifted with his mouth. Vestal virgins couldn't—wouldn't— resist his sweet assault. Bright light flooded through her closed eyes, exploding in tiny bursts of white. Sensation pooled and built between her legs. His tongue sampled and seduced, bringing her to new heights of pleasure. If her pussy had swelled and shuddered, her ass tingled and trembled. His tongue felt like hot liquid teasing its way past the tight ring of muscle to dazzle her inner walls. If she could have pulled him in deeper, trapped him there, she would have. But the sensation was too exquisite, the fever running too high. He pushed one finger inside her ass and one inside her pussy, intensifying the pleasure a thousandfold. The ceiling above her spiraled out of sight, and the couch below her vanished. He chose that moment to run his tongue over her clit, and once again she broke around him. Her body spasmed out of control. The air was whipped from her lungs. She spun weightless in the air, connected to earth only by the sinful hand and mouth of Gabriel Carter, lover extraordinaire.

And when the climax receded she collapsed backward onto the couch, bamboozled.

Strong arms lifted her from her resting place and carried her through her flat. The soft cotton of her bedspread cushioned her butt as Gabe laid her on the bed.

She pushed herself up into a sitting position, trying to make sense of the last few minutes, but Gabe was having none of it.

"I'm not done yet," he told her, his voice deeper than usual and a little breathless. "I intend to make you come again. At least twice more. But this time I won't use my fingers or my mouth. This time you'll find your pleasure in a very different way."

As he spoke, he unbuttoned her blouse and pushed it off her. Then he unclipped her bra and tossed that aside so she lay naked before him. He swallowed as he took in her naked body, his eyes sweeping over her.

"Gabe..." Her voice trailed off. She had no idea what to say to him. She should tell him to stop, but God help her, she didn't want him to. What she wanted were those other orgasms he promised her.

"Christ, T. You've got me so aroused I'm ready to burst a nut here." He undid the buttons of his jeans and twisted the waist. "Pants...too bloody...tight," he gasped. "I want so badly to fuck you. I want to slide into your pussy and lose myself in your body. Like I used to. Want it so bad I can almost feel your wet heat around my dick." Gabe closed his eyes for a second and grimaced.

Tina moaned. God, she wanted that too. Wanted Gabe to press his glorious cock inside her. Wanted him to fuck her like he used to, until she came, screaming his name—or Connor's—in sheer ecstasy. She bent her knees and drew her thighs apart, her legs preparing for the sensual onslaught.

Gabe ran his finger over her engorged clit and swore. "Not gonna do it," he said in a strained voice. "Not gonna hurt you again."

Tina's heart dropped even as sensation charged through her pussy. He'd promised her more orgasms!

He played with her clit, tracing tiny circles around it with his huge finger. "But I am gonna make you come. And I'm going to watch as every tremor wracks your body. I'm going to watch as your nipples harden into tight buds and your skin breaks out in goose bumps."

Tina gulped. When it came to sex she had no doubt Gabe would follow through on every promise. But if he wasn't going to fuck her then how—

"May I open the drawer beside your bed?" He dipped his finger between her pussy lips and drew it back up over her clit.

Ah! Waves of heat flooded through her as she nodded. The goose bumps he'd just mentioned began to creep up her back and over her arms.

"Close your eyes, T," he instructed, his fingers still seducing her.

Her lids drifted shut.

Gabe pulled away from her, leaving behind a dull, empty ache where his hand had been. She heard the soft rumble of the drawer opening and then the sounds of plastic knocking against wood and glass pinging against glass.

And then there was silence.

"Perfect," he whispered.

She did not need to look to know he wore a satisfied smile. She clenched her thighs together as her pussy began to throb. Oh, Lord. What had he found? What had he chosen?

"Your collection has grown," he said, clearly impressed. The mattress dipped, and denim brushed against her leg. "But I think for today we can settle on your old friend."

Tina shivered. She knew exactly who the old friend was. Her trusted rabbit pal. Not the very same one Gabe and Connor had used on her before, but a close relative nevertheless. Moisture gathered between her legs, her body preparing itself for the exquisite torture she knew would follow.

A hand on her knee pushed her legs apart again. "Because sometimes," he whispered, "it's the old friends who bring you the most pleasure." Something cool and wet brushed over her groin, and her muscles clenched. Then came the soft whirring.

Tina shuddered as a vibrating jellied tip touched her clit, sending sharp sparks of delight shooting through her. She groaned and then sagged as the rabbit was pulled away. The vibrations ceased, although the soft whir did not. Less than a second later her body convulsed as the tip touched her lower lips. The tremors tantalized her, leaving her achy and needy. She wanted more. Wanted the rabbit inside. She moaned and twisted her hips, and Gabe obliged.

He slid the toy into her channel, pushing and stretching her, teasing and taunting her. The gentle buzzing drove her crazy, sweet torment against the walls of her pussy. Sweet that was, until the vibrations increased in speed. And then need overcame her. She pushed back down on the rabbit, pushed against Gabe's hand, wanting more, needing release.

"Ah, T." Gabe's voice felt like a million prickles down her spine. "Always so responsive."

Another change. Different movement. He'd turned on the beads, and they rotated around and around, pulsating through her pussy, making her cry out.

"That's it, sweetness," Gabe urged. "Take all the pleasure you need."

She clenched her muscles around the toy, squeezing as hard as she could, slowing the movement down. And then she relaxed again, giving the rabbit free rein. It was all she could take. Blood thrummed in her ears, her legs shook and an orgasm blindsided her, leaving her breathless.

"Ah, Christ!" Gabe sounded as breathless as she felt. "God, I love to watch you come. Love when...your pussy...shudders. Your clit..." He moaned. "Fuck, I want to lick your clit."

Her hips buckled as he drove the rabbit higher, increasing the speed of rotation. Silver light ripped through her as the tiny quivering ears touched her swollen bud, and a fresh set of tremors shook her. Still he didn't stop, just kept the toy whirring, kept her body flying until she turned her head and sobbed into her pillow, the pleasure too intense—almost painful. Just when she thought she couldn't stand it anymore, he slipped a finger in her ass and bit the tender skin of her inner thigh.

Tina dissolved. She knew nothing but the torrents of wicked rapture flooding her veins.

Gabe sat statue still at base of the bed, forcing himself not to move. If he so much as breathed now, he would not be able to stem the tide of his desire. He would rip of his clothes, lunge at Tina and drive himself—unprotected—into the writhing depths of her pussy.

He clenched his eyes shut, bit down hard on his tongue

and counted to thirty. Sweat beaded on his forehead and dripped down his back. His balls smarted with unreleased tension, his dick so hard the pain cut through him.

Christ, he needed relief. He needed to come.

Not here. Not now.

This was not about him. It was about Tina. About proving to her that even though he'd left her once, he was back now. Back to prove he would do anything, everything for her. He would shift the world if he could to please her. Move planets. Realign the stars.

A low moan snapped him from his reverie, and carefully, cautiously, he turned the vibe off and slid it out of Tina. She collapsed in a spent heap before him, her chest heaving.

Gabe inched off the bed and knelt on the floor beside the head of the mattress. Every action was a challenge. He ached so damn bad, spasms tore through his abdomen.

She turned to stare at him, her brown eyes enormous in her passion-glazed face.

"Earlier you wanted to know if I'd kissed you because I love you." He growled in her ear. "The answer is yes."

Confusion clouded her irises. "Wha...?"

"I do love you. I have since the day Connor introduced us." As he spoke, certainty of his feelings pushed forward in his mind. Four years may have passed. They did not dampen the intensity of his love for her one iota.

"But you...you left us. You left...me." Her voice was breathless.

"Because you were with him first. I couldn't have you." He bit back his resentment. Connor wasn't to blame for the course of events that had pushed him away from Tina. Their code of honor was. If not for Connor he'd never even have met Tina.

"You did have me, Gabe. You and Connor—you had all of me. I loved you both. So very much."

Glass cut at his heart. The erection that had been plaguing him died a sudden death. "You loved us...both?"

She closed her eyes on a sigh. "With everything I had. You two were my life."

The glass sliced deeper. Her love was a mixed blessing. How could he make her his own if she'd loved Connor as well? "I couldn't share you." Gabe's voice was hoarse. The words scraped his throat. "Not once I knew I loved you."

"Gabe..."

"Every time Connor was with you I wanted to tear him apart, one limb at a time." The last time they'd made love to her, he'd hated Connor with every cell in his body. Every time his friend touched Tina, Gabe had seen red. It had been the most agonizing sexual experience of his life, being with the woman he loved and watching his best friend fuck her at the same time. "I had to leave, T. It was either that or knock Connor unconscious." He clenched his fist at his side.

Her gaze darted to his hand. "Y-you...never said anything."

Gabe shook his head. What the fuck could he have said that wouldn't have destroyed his and Connor's friendship, or Tina and Connor's relationship?

He made a concerted effort to relax the muscles in his hand and straighten his fingers. "We had our rules. I couldn't breach them. I couldn't betray Connor that way."

Tina scooched up the bed and dragged the covers over her naked body. She clutched the doona tight around her breasts while laughing cynically. "Oh, so it was okay for Connor to break the rules to be with Maggie, but not for you to break the rules to be with me."

"Maddie," he corrected and squeezed his eyes shut for a second. Shit, his explanation had come out sounding all wrong. Instead of clearing up the circumstances with her, he'd made it worse. "Connor never broke the rules. I did."

She frowned at him. "What is that supposed to mean?"

"When Connor realized he had feelings for Maddie, he tried to walk away. He did it because of the rules. He did it to save our friendship." Gabe hesitated. "I wouldn't let him."

"*You* wouldn't let him?" Again with the reproachful stare.

"I've been there, T. I know what it's like to walk away from the woman you love. I fucked up with you. I wasn't about to let Connor make the same mistake with Maddie."

Tina flashed him a sweet smile. "Ah, Gabe, what a hero. Gosh, Maggie and Connor must be ever so grateful for your self-sacrificing ways."

Gabe considered correcting Tina for the third time, but one look at her face told him the use of the wrong name was intentional. She knew good and well what Maddie's name was. "I didn't just do it for them," he confessed. "My intentions were selfish."

She eyed him with suspicion.

"Seeing Connor and Maddie together? It brought back all the old feelings. Reminded me, again, of how damn much I loved you. I didn't want Maddie. I wanted you." He shrugged, although there was nothing blasé about the way he felt. "I always have." His heart pumped overtime, and a cold sweat formed on his back. "I came to tell you that, came to see if there was any chance you could reciprocate that love." He swallowed, terrified of her response.

Tina's expression turned hard. "You're about four years too late, don't you think?"

"I know it's been a while."

She snorted. "A while? You classify four years as a while?"

"I classify it as a fucking eternity. Forty-eight months. Or, in our case, forty-nine months, two weeks and one day." And not one of those days or weeks or months had passed without Gabe missing her. "But who's counting?"

Her shoulders seemed to sag. "Obviously you are."

"I'm not kidding about this, T. I love you. I've been in love with you all this time." Gabe almost laughed out loud at the irony. How was it possible that a mere slip of a woman could wield such power over him? Could hold his happiness in her hands?

"So why did you wait so long to tell me?" She shrugged helplessly. "I don't understand. Why didn't you come back ages ago?"

"God knows I wanted to." Gabe jumped up. "So much. It killed me, knowing you lived so close and I couldn't have you." He began to pace. "I left Sydney for a while. Six months."

Tina's gaze followed him as he paced the length of the room. "Where did you go?"

"Europe."

"What about your job?"

"I resigned. Gave up the lease on my house too."

"To get away for me?"

"You and Connor," he corrected.

"And when you came back? Three and a half years ago?" The accusation was implicit in her question.

Gabe stood still and looked at her. "I still loved you." He brushed a hand over his face. "I wanted to come to you the day my flight landed. The day Connor told me you and he had split up."

"So why the hell didn't you?"

Gabe stared at her for a long time. "I did. That night." Armed with a massive bunch of roses and a keen willingness to beg her to love him.

"Gee, Gabe, I think I'd have remembered if you'd shown up at my doorstep."

"You weren't home," he told her tonelessly.

"Ah." She nodded. "So you tried once, had no luck and gave up. It never occurred to you to come back the next day? Or the day after that?"

"You weren't here, but your sister was."

Tina narrowed her eyes.

"Seems Leanne and Michael were staying here for the week." It hurt just to remember. Christ, he was turning into a pussy.

Tina nodded as her eyes filled with comprehension. "Their place was being painted. They moved in while I was away with…" Her voice trailed off.

"With your new boyfriend," Gabe supplied. The boyfriend Tina was head-over-heels in love with. The boyfriend who Leanne was quick to point out, was sure to become the fiancé. The boyfriend who put a stop to all Gabe's whimsical fantasies about Tina, although the two men never met.

"Grant," Tina said, voicing the name he never wanted to hear again.

"I would have come back," Gabe told her. "Every night if need be. But your sister said you were happy, said he was the real deal. It wasn't fair for me to interfere."

"So you left," she murmured, more to herself than to him.

"So I left," he agreed and let that hang between them for a while. "Is he the same guy?" Gabe asked after a moment.

She looked confused. "Same as what?"

"Is he the one you kissed in the coffee shop today?"

"God, no." She wrinkled her nose. "No, Grant and I didn't last more than a couple of months."

"And the one this morning?"

"Less than that," Tina said. "He wasn't right from the start."

Gabe stood up and paced the room, gritting his teeth to stop from swearing. He'd given Tina up for a relationship that had lasted a few fucking months? If the wall had been closer, he would have banged his head against it, hard. Fuck, what a waste of time. He could have had her for the last three and a half years. Instead he'd taken Leanne's advice and walked away. Pretended to be the hero. And wound up lonely instead. He'd felt uprooted and alone in a city he'd lived in his whole life.

Instead of fighting for Tina, like every instinct had dictated, he'd thrown himself into creating new roots. He'd bought a flat. The first property he'd ever owned. And he'd begun his own private practice rather than working for someone else. The new home and the practice had helped provide him with some stability, but they'd never eased the ache or the loneliness of not being with the woman he loved.

"I don't get it." Tina looked at him, puzzled. "Why did you walk away three years ago when you found out I was with someone else, yet you hung around today after seeing me kiss Anthony?"

"Because three years ago you were happy." Or so Leanne had said anyway. "Today you looked miserable. I couldn't just leave." Ah hell, why not just tell her the full truth? "I didn't want to leave. Not again. I wanted to see you, speak to you. I wanted another chance."

Tina dropped her head in her hands, covering her face. "Why are you telling me all this now? What do you want from me?"

Once again Gabe dropped to his knees beside the head of her bed. "I want everything, T. I want to be with you, just the two of us. No one else to complicate our relationship. I want another chance to prove you can fall in love with me and me alone."

Tina shook her head. "Stop!" She threw out a hand to punctuate her plea and turned to him with tear-filled eyes. "Please, stop. It's been too long, Gabe. Too much has happened. I... I'm too angry with you to go down this road." She took a deep, rasping breath. "You l-left me. You left us. When I was with you and Connor I was so happy. You became my life, my rocks. And y-yes, I loved you then, but it's not quite as simple as that." She took a deep, shuddering breath. "I loved you b-both. Together." She wrinkled her nose in concentration. "I can't separate you from Connor, and I can't separate my feelings for you from my feelings for Connor. When I think of you I think of Connor, and when I think of Connor I think of you."

She drummed the palm of her hand against her forehead in frustration. "You destroyed that. When you walked out on Connor and me you destroyed our threesome. You broke up my life and you tore out my heart. Connor and I couldn't go on without you. We weren't whole anymore."

Her words ripped through his chest. Christ, she couldn't distinguish him from Connor. Couldn't separate them out in her mind. He hadn't stood out enough as an individual. He was simply one half of a whole.

He wasn't man enough for the one woman he wanted to spend the rest of his life with.

Gabe rose to his feet, the weight of his realization sitting like lead on his shoulders. "I'm sorry I hurt you," he said. "And I'm sorry I broke up your life. It was never my intention to cause you pain. Please. Give me a chance to make it right. Let me prove that I can love you enough for Connor and me. Love you enough that you'll forgive my leaving you before."

Tina shook her head. "I can't do it, Gabe. I can't pretend I'd be okay with just you. If—and that's a big 'if'—I ever did consider becoming involved with you again, I'd want the whole package deal. I'd want you *and* Connor." Tears stood out in her eyes. "But it's been too long anyway. Too much time has passed for me to ever go back."

Gabe buttoned his jeans and straightened his shirt, the pain of her admission strangling him, cutting off his air. He took a deep, ragged breath. Tried to put his thoughts in order. Tried to maintain a modicum of composure. Not easy when he felt like he'd just been kicked in the nuts.

He gave her a small nod. "I hear you, T. And I guess I owe you yet another apology. I...it was wrong of me to seek you out after all this time. Forget about today. Forget about me and everything I told you." He took another ragged breath. "I hope I haven't upset you. I...I won't bother you anymore." He walked towards the door, his legs stiff and awkward. "Good luck with the exhibition. I'm sure with Valerie's help your sketches will finally get the recognition they deserve."

"You're leaving?" She gaped at him.

Gabe nodded.

"After everything you just said to me? Everything you just did to me?" She kicked the covers, and the vibrator rolled off the bed and landed on the floor with a soft thud.

Gabe stared at it for a long moment. "I had to try. I had to let you know how I felt, on the off chance that maybe you felt the same." He shrugged indifferently while inside his stomach cramped. "It would have been good if we could have tried again, just the two of us. But I'm not what you want anymore. I'm just...a man. Just one man. And that's all I'll ever be."

And then he couldn't be with her any longer. Couldn't face his failure to please her as that one man. He'd disappointed her when he'd left her the first time, and he hadn't measured up this time round. It would be better for both of them if he just left her the hell alone.

"Goodbye, Tina," he said as he walked through the bedroom door. "Be happy."

Chapter Five

Inadequate. Not the best way to think of oneself, was it? But that's how Gabe felt as he walked into his kitchen when he arrived home. Always used to being in control when it came to women, he was thrown by this situation. He wasn't man enough for the woman he loved. Alone he couldn't measure up to what Tina wanted.

He stopped short when he saw Connor standing by the kettle, a steaming mug in his hands.

"Hey," Gabe said by way of greeting. "I thought you were heading back to Melbourne about now?"

Connor nodded. "My flight leaves in a couple of hours. I wanted to catch you and say goodbye."

Gabe looked at him speculatively. "Where's Maddie?"

Connor pointed his thumb over his shoulder. "In the living room."

Gabe nodded. "Did you two work everything out?"

Connor grinned. "We sure did."

He smiled back. "Maddie's good for you. I'm happy for you both." He was. It didn't stop the twist of jealousy in his gut. Connor had found the perfect partner. A woman who wanted just Connor.

Gabe's perfect partner wanted more than Gabe. She wanted

Connor too.

Connor nodded in agreement. "I've decided to come back to Sydney."

"You going to take up the job offer after all?" Connor had been in town this weekend to interview for a position. He'd been undecided about returning to Sydney. Maddie must have helped him make up his mind.

"Yep."

"That's cool." It would be nice to have his mate back in the same city again. "When d'ya think you'll make the move?"

Connor took his mug and sat at the kitchen table. "Two months, max. I'll have to find someone to replace me at work and train them up before I can leave."

"You going to see Maddie in the interim?"

"Damn straight," Connor said. "I'll visit here and she'll come to Melbourne. We'll alternate weekends."

"Sounds like a plan." Christ, it was difficult to believe that a few days ago Maddie was with Gabe, and Connor had just entered the picture. Life had spun around almost one hundred and eighty degrees since then.

"Gabe?"

"Yeah?"

"I owe you a thank you."

Gabe raised an eyebrow in question.

"If not for you, I'd be in Melbourne, and Maddie and I never would have gotten together."

"Don't mention it." Gabe shrugged. Maddie and Connor made a good couple. "True love doesn't come around often. No point wasting it."

"Yeah." Connor frowned. "That's the other reason I'm here."

Gabe's lips tilted in a smile. "You going to tell me you've been in love with me all this time?"

Connor snorted. "Yeah, right!" And then he became serious. "I wanted to apologize."

"For what?" Gabe asked, puzzled. "If this is about you and Maddie, there's no need. You were meant to be together."

"It's not about me. Or Maddie. I'm sorry I never broke the rules four years ago."

Gabe stood stock still.

"You loved Tina. I should have realized then just how much and walked away."

"I never expected you to. She was yours first. We had rules."

"Yeah, that's the thing." Connor scraped his fingers through his hair. "I was too rigid in the way I stuck to the rules. I can see that now. Trying to leave Maddie just about killed me. I can imagine what saying goodbye to Tina did to you."

Ripped out his heart and shredded it. "It hurt," Gabe acknowledged. It still hurt, maybe even more now.

Connor shook his head. Remorse lined his face. "I fucked up, mate. I should have cut her loose the minute I understood how much it messed with your head when we both slept with her."

"I left. There was no need to cut her loose."

"You left because I didn't," Connor pointed out. "I fucked up."

"I did too," Gabe said after a minute. "I could have tried harder to win her over. I didn't."

"Do you still love her?"

Gabe sighed. "Uh huh." Not that it made a difference now.

Connor studied him for a few seconds. "You look like shite."

"Thanks, mate." Gabe almost laughed.

"Did you find her?"

He poured himself a mug of coffee. "Yeah. She was at the coffee shop on the corner."

Connor waited until Gabe sat opposite him at the table before asking, "And?"

Gabe shook his head. "And nothing."

"Nothing?" Connor narrowed his eyes.

"She's not interested."

"You're kidding, right?"

"Wish I was." Gabe dropped his hands on the table. Damn, he wished he was.

"Is she involved with anyone?"

"Not anymore. She broke it off this morning."

"How'd she respond to seeing you again?"

Gabe thought about the answer. "She was surprised at first, but forced herself to make small talk for a few minutes. Then she threw in a couple of sarcastic comments for good measure and walked away."

Connor stared at him in disbelief. "And you let her go?"

"Fuck, no! I went after her. We spent a little time together." Memories of the time raced through his mind, the images of her naked and convulsing in pleasure blindsiding him.

"Christ, Carter." Connor chuckled. "You slept with her."

Gabe grimaced. "Nah, mate. I didn't. Wanted to, real bad, but never did."

"So why the look on your face?"

That was the problem about sleeping with the same woman at the same time as your best friend. You couldn't hide your sexual exploits from him when he knew you so well. "Things got heated. That's all."

"You saying you got T all hot and worked up and nothing came of it?" Connor frowned. "Doesn't sound like the woman I remember. Doesn't sound like you either, for that matter."

Gabe took a mouthful of coffee. How much did he tell Connor? Sure, they'd always shared everything when it came to Tina. That's how he'd gotten into this screwed-up situation in the first place. But now they'd gone their different paths. Connor had chosen Maddie, and Gabe had chosen Tina. They were no longer partners on a sexual journey. From this point on they both flew solo.

Well, Connor had Maddie. It was just Gabe flying solo.

Still, he needed a friend, and Connor was the one guy he'd trusted his whole life. He'd leave out the details about Tina getting naked, but the rest he could speak to Connor about. "I'm screwed," he said after another minute's deliberation. "When it comes to matters of the heart, I am good and fucked." He slammed his mug on the table. Dark drops of liquids splashed over the sides and onto the wooden surface.

Connor jerked in surprise. "What happened between the two of you?"

"I spoke pretty frankly with her. Told her I left because I loved her."

"And...?"

"And she told me that four years ago she loved me too. Me and you."

Connor swore. "Both of us?"

"She thinks of us as a single entity. Two halves of a whole."

Connor twisted his lips as he digested that bit of information. "Fuck me," he muttered.

They sat in silence for several moments.

"Think it was the same for all of them?" Gabe asked. "We know Maddie didn't have that outlook. But what about the others?"

Connor shrugged. "Until Maddie I'd never thought about our threesomes in terms of love. They were fun, sure. And satisfying. But love?" He shook his head. "It was never part of the equation for me. I'd never contemplated a love relationship with three of us."

Gabe grimaced. "Me neither." Especially not when it came to Tina. "Maybe I'm naïve, but I don't think it was a question of love with the others. I think they were in it for the same reasons as we were. Sexual exploration and sexual gratification."

Connor nodded. "Tina and Maddie are the only two who stand out as acting differently."

"Maybe we were the ones acting differently with Tina and Maddie?"

"Because we loved them."

Connor let out a long sigh. "What are you going to do now?"

"Fuck if I know," Gabe told him.

"There's only one thing you can do," a feminine voice said from behind Gabe.

Connor's gaze swung above Gabe's head.

Gabe twisted around to see Maddie standing in the doorway.

She gave him a quick smile and answered his silent question. "I thought I'd wait in the living room while Connor and you spoke in private. I... I didn't mean to eavesdrop, but I couldn't help but overhear your conversation."

Maddie glowed. She had a gleam to her eyes that he'd never seen before. A gleam that Connor had reflected when he'd looked up at her. Gabe tried to ignore the tightening in his chest. He wasn't jealous of Connor's relationship with his ex-girlfriend. He *was* envious of the love that flowed between them.

"You have to go after her, Gabe," Maddie said with conviction. "You have to prove to her that you are man enough for any woman."

Gabe laughed out loud at her words, although they were not amusing. "Just like I proved I was man enough for you?" Christ, talk about his ego taking a knock. Dumped by Maddie in favor of Connor in the wee hours of the morning and rejected by Tina not twelve hours later. Ah, yes, Gabe felt as much a man as a castrated bull might.

Maddie pointed her finger at him. "You were more than man enough for me, Gabriel Carter. Hell, you did things to me no one has ever done before. You ignited fires I never knew could be lit."

Connor growled at her from across the table.

"Hush, Connor," Maddie chided. "You know what Gabe did to me. You were there when he did it. You encouraged him to do it."

Connor made a strangled sound but said nothing. Gabe appreciated the effort it must have taken.

"My point is, Gabe," Maddie continued, "I've been alone with you, and I can say with complete confidence that you are all any woman would need. Tina may have once loved both of you, but she never got to know you alone. I'm not surprised she fell for you *and* Connor. You presented yourselves as a package deal. When you left, Gabe, the relationship didn't last. Without you, Connor and Tina didn't work anymore."

Yep, and Tina had made it crystal clear that without Connor she and Gabe wouldn't work either.

"You have a dubious look on your face," Maddie informed

73

Gabe. "Get rid of it." She walked to the table and took a seat between Connor and Gabe. She took Gabe's hand.

"Maddie..." Connor objected, but she silenced him with a look.

Gabe gave him an apologetic smile. He knew how he'd feel if Tina took Connor's hand now.

Maddie continued as if no silent communication had passed between the two men. "The Gabe I know would not doubt his ability to woo a woman. You charmed me and seduced me all by yourself. You gave me a chance to get to know you before Connor entered the picture. Yes, it's true that when I met Connor I fell for him. I chose him. But Tina didn't. She had her chance with Connor after you left, and she gave it up. What she never had a chance at was getting to know you separately from Connor. Getting to choose you."

His heart twisted again. "I gave her that chance this morning. She wasn't interested."

"That's bullshit," Maddie said. "How can you expect her to say anything else? After four years of complete silence you surprise her with an admission of love. You think she's going to throw herself in your arms and confess her undying love for you? Not a chance, buddy. You dumped her. You walked away. And I'm betting you hurt her in the process. No way she's going to come running back to you after all that."

Gabe remained silent. There was little he could say in defense. Heck, Maddie was right on every count.

"Go after her. Go show her the real you. The individual. The man separate from Connor."

"She's right, Carter," Connor said. "You owe it to yourself and to her. Give yourselves a chance to get to know each other."

"C'mon," Maddie said, "you told me yourself not a day goes

by when you don't think about her. Don't let another day pass like that. Act now."

Gabe remained silent.

"Damn it, Gabe!" Maddie yelled at him. "How can you be so dominant in bed and so fucking useless out of it? So what if she rebuffed you once? Go prove you're bigger than that. A real man would not run away at the first hint of trouble."

Gabe's spine stiffened. Until today his masculinity had never been questioned. He'd never questioned it. Now Tina had him doubting himself.

"How badly do you want her?" Connor asked.

"How badly did you want Maddie?" Gabe shot back at him.

Connor grimaced and nodded. "A damn lot."

"Well, multiply that by four years and you might have an inkling."

"Gabe," Maddie said beside him. "Go get your girl. Go and prove to Tina that you are all the man she'll ever need."

Gabe stared at Maddie for a very long time.

"Do it, Carter," Connor encouraged. "Pull out all the stops. Go and get your girl."

Gabe squared his shoulders. Since when did one knock back mean he had to stop trying? Gabe was not the kind of guy who gave up without a fight, not when his goals meant something to him. And Tina meant something. Heck, Tina meant everything.

And that was all the decision time he needed.

Gabe leaned over and kissed Maddie on the cheek. Then he walked around the table to clap Connor on the back. "Mate," he said to his friend, "you're damn lucky Maddie loves you. If I wasn't so hell-bent on winning Tina over, I'd pull out all the stops to get Maddie back." He winked at Maddie who rolled her eyes in response. "Now if you'll both excuse me, I have a woman to woo."

Chapter Six

Tina stared in disbelief at the hulking mountain of a man standing in her doorway. *He'd come back.* After the way he'd left earlier, she'd believed he'd never want to lay eyes on her again.

An intense wave of relief swept over her.

"Have dinner with me?" he invited, as if nothing had transpired between the two of them today. As if he hadn't professed his love for her. As if he hadn't brought her to orgasm several times over. As if she hadn't watched his face shadow over when she'd told him she'd loved both him and Connor.

"Y-you want to have a meal together?"

He shrugged. "We both have to eat."

Tina hoped her jaw hadn't dropped in response. Two hours ago Gabe had left with a tortured look on his face. Now he was extending a casual invitation to dinner.

She said the first thing that came to mind. "Well, gosh, Gabe. I'm kinda busy right now. You know? Forgetting about you and forgetting about today. Just like you instructed. I don't have the time to stop for a bite."

Gabe's answering smile was slow to develop. "Damn, T, maybe one day I'll learn to take offense to your cynical nature."

"Damn, G, maybe one day you won't inspire cynicism in me."

He nodded, every glimmer of his smile gone. "I can only hope. May I come in?"

She narrowed her eyes as she looked up at him belligerently. "That depends. Do you have any plans to raid the contents of my bedside drawer again?" Her stomach gave an unexpected quiver. Shit. She should know better than to refer to her toys. Gabe's skill with a vibrator surpassed any man's she'd known, even Connor's.

A muscle ticked in his jaw. "That would—" Gabe shook his head and broke off mid-sentence. "I came to take you to dinner, that's it." He frowned. "I swear there will not be a repeat of this afternoon's performance..." This time he let his words trail off.

Tina eyed him warily. He'd left way too much unsaid. He could have finished his sentence with...*unless you want there to be one.* And damn it, she did. Just standing opposite Gabe had her nerves jumping about in a state of useless confusion. Okay, not confusion. Longing. Being anywhere near the man brought out a deep-seated ache for the physical gratification he and Connor had once freely provided.

She pushed the lust aside. Five orgasms and a confession of love in one day was about as much as her body could handle. Or her mind, for that matter.

Lord, where'd Gabe learn how to do all of that? He was the only man she knew who could bring her to orgasm more than once in a single session of lovemaking. Even Connor, for all his skill, hadn't had the ability. But Gabe. Damn, over and over again she came for him, until her body was limp and sated and exhausted.

With less reluctance than she would have liked, Tina stepped aside and let him in. She'd have to take him at his word. Gabe may have done a lot of things, but he'd never lied. If he swore nothing would happen, nothing would happen.

Unless, of course, *she* changed the rules.

She gave a sharp mental shake of her head. She wouldn't.

He walked into her flat, and she closed the door behind them. That was when the momentary panic set in. Christ, he was back. Now what? Did she have to relive old memories once again? The months when she was happiest with the men she loved? The days when nothing could have gotten her down because she had two gorgeous men whom she adored and who worshipped her?

At first it had been just her and Connor. That had been fun. Connor was a smart guy with a wicked sense of humor. Sleeping with him was a serious turn-on. Then Gabe entered the equation, and the sex had gone from good to explosive. Making love to Connor *and* Gabe was the most sensual, most satisfying, most thrilling experience of her life. Falling in love with them had been a natural progression in their relationship. If the choice had been hers, she would have stayed with both of them forever.

The choice hadn't been hers. Gabe had left, destroying the most precious of bonds.

She thumped him on the back. Hard.

"Ugh!" He turned in surprise. "What was that for?"

"For walking out on me. On us." She glowered at him, anger settling in the pit of her stomach.

"So you hit me?"

"Hit? Hah, I'd beat you senseless if I knew I stood a chance."

His pupils dilated. "You stand every chance. Don't you know you've rendered me senseless on more than one occasion?"

"Bull," she sneered. "I've never even punched you before."

She corrected her error now, clenching her fist and striking out as hard as she could. Her hand connected with his stomach, and her breath left her body in a gasp. Damn it! She'd hit a wall of solid muscle, and the only pain she'd caused was to her own fingers.

Gabe gawked at her. "You don't need to punch me. Just being with you takes my breath away." He dropped his gaze to his stomach and then lifted it back up to meet hers again. His tone was lowered by several notches. "Making love to you... Damn, I never could think straight when I was inside you. Couldn't see, couldn't hear." Gabe closed his eyes on a groan. "All I could do was feel."

His words rolled through her like warm honey, slipping through her veins, heating her blood. "Shut up, Gabe." Pain be damned. She punched him again and then again, this time on his arm. "I'm busy being pissed off at you."

He tensed his biceps, accepting her blows without comment.

Shit, wasn't that just typical Gabe behavior? Everything went by without comment. Everything. Even his departure from her life. She hit him harder. Then harder again. "Damn you, Gabriel Carter," she spluttered. "You left us. You left me. You walked away from the best thing that ever happened to me. You bastard." The hand she'd been attacking with throbbed so she switched arms and pummeled him good. Rage came bubbling to the surface, lending strength to her strikes. "I loved you, goddamn it. You and Connor. You were my world. My happiness. And. You. Walked. Away. You destroyed us."

Four years, and who would have thought she still had so much emotion left in her? So much bloody anger and despair. Yes, he may have come back six months later, but by then it was already too late. She'd met Grant and tried to move on with her life.

"I destroyed me too," Gabe whispered.

"Shut up," she snapped. "You don't get to have a say now. You don't get to tell me how you felt. You're four years too bloody late for that."

She raised her arm to strike him again, but before her hand found its target, he acted. In less time than it took to blink, Tina hung suspended in space, her legs dangling uselessly below her. Gabe had her caught between his body and the wall. His chest pressed into hers, flattening her breasts against his pecs, against a barrier of super hard male flesh. His thigh was wedged between her legs, holding her up, pushing against her groin, making even the slightest move an exquisite form of torture. And his mouth was inches, centimeters, from hers. So close the rasping heat of his breath warmed her lips, tickled her nose and sent a blast of half-crazed lust careening down her spine.

"You were my world, T. But you were Connor's first. I didn't have a choice." He thrust his thigh up, and she battled against him.

Oh, holy hell. She needed to stop struggling. The sensations smashing through her and lighting up her core had her writhing with need. Either she had to quit struggling—or she needed to go to war with him. All-out war, which would have only one result. An orgasm. And a damn hard one if her current state of desire was anything to go by.

"We all have choices," she bit back and then added for good measure, "Sometimes we just make the wrong ones."

"You think I don't know how bad my decision was?" Gabe's voice was hoarse, the look in his eyes tortured. "You think I didn't spend the last three and a half years in hell wondering how you were? If you were married? Happy?" He ground his thigh against her pussy, and she bit back a whimper. "You think this is what I want? My leg here? Fuck, T, I want my whole body between your legs. I want..." He closed his eyes and groaned. "I want to be inside you. So goddamned deep inside you I lose myself. I want...need to feel your warm pussy wrapped around me, pulling me in deeper and deeper..."

Tina gulped, because now that he'd voiced it out loud, she wanted the very same thing. She had a maddening compulsion to tear off her clothes and his, draw him down to the floor and envelop his hard length with her pussy.

He dropped his head, resting his forehead against hers, taking in great gulps of air. She sucked in the air he exhaled, greedy for anything of his to become a part of her.

His voice was erotic as sin as he panted out, "Need to...make love...to you."

She dissolved. Any reluctance that might have prevented her from responding dissipated in his words, in his raw desire for her. Her eyelids drooped, her lips parted, and she raised her chin to meet his mouth in the inevitability of a kiss. More than her next breath, she wanted his mouth on hers.

Which made the resounding thud beside her left ear all the more shocking.

Gabe pounded the wall with his fist. Once, twice and a third time. With a strangled moan he dropped his thigh and drew away from Tina. He did not release her until her feet touched the ground.

With legs as useless as rubber, she slid weightlessly down the wall, her knees caving beneath her, and came to rest in a shapeless lump on the carpeted floor.

Gabe prowled her lounge, a veritable giant amongst her furniture. He drew to a halt against the wall opposite her, hit it once and then dropped to the floor as well.

For endless moments he stared at her, his eyes hooded, his mouth drawn. The sound of heavy breathing echoed in her ears. His? Hers? She had no idea. Her heart slammed into her ribs, her lungs seeking oxygen in the airless room.

"I'm sorry," he rasped. "I...shouldn't have done that."

She waited until she was sure she could string a sentence together. "I...shouldn't have hit you." Yet even with the acknowledgement her hand still curled into a fist, the dull ache in her knuckles nothing compared to the need to lash out at him again.

He stared at her fist and raised an eyebrow. The look on his face might have been skeptical—if longing and naked desire hadn't shadowed his eyes. "But you're not sorry you did."

She forced her fingers to straighten. "You hurt me, Gabe."

He nodded. "I'm sorry."

"I wanted to...hurt you back."

Another nod. "That's okay." He slumped against the wall and let his arms drop to his sides. "I won't respond this time. I swear." He kept his gaze level with hers. "Come at me. Hurt me as much as you need to."

Instinct made her hands curl into fists again, but this time, Tina restrained herself. If she went at him now she'd last maybe three seconds before her blows turned to caresses. Instead of inflicting pain she'd draw relief from touching his skin. If she so much as tapped a finger to his flesh now, she'd be naked and begging for more before Gabe had time to register what had—or hadn't—hit him.

She bit back a frustrated cry. "I just want..." Her voice trailed off. "I want... I need..." She shook her head, unable to put words to her thoughts.

"What is it, T? Tell me. Anything you want. Anything. It's

yours."

She shook her head, her eyes filling with tears. "I just want..." And then because nothing else would have made sense under the circumstances, she said, "I just want pasta for dinner."

They went to an Italian restaurant. Gabe plied her with good food and good wine. He entertained her with stories about his patients and his practice. He coaxed her into telling him about her life over the last few years, listening to each word as if he were hungry to discover every detail he'd missed. So enjoyable was his company she was almost lulled into believing the incident in her apartment had never taken place. Almost. Except for the tangible desire Gabe seemed to emit with every breath.

The heat between them pinged back and forth across the table, Gabe exhaling it, she inhaling. It burned through her lungs as clearly as if he'd touched her, scorching her with his fingers. He *hadn't* touched her. Not once. There had been no physical contact between them since he'd released her from the sensual prison of his body. Didn't mean she wasn't aware of the lust that hissed between them.

As she spoke he watched her with heavy-lidded eyes. Each time she laughed his gaze lingered on her mouth for just a second too long. The one time she'd licked a drop of Neapolitan sauce from her lip, his lips had parted, the bottom one pink and full, as though it had just been kissed.

And then there were the not-so-subtle hints. The blatant expressions of his need that whipped up a whirlwind in her stomach and made eating impossible.

"T," he whispered when there was a lull in conversation.

She leaned forward to hear him better. "Yes, Gabe?"

"I want to strip every single item of clothing from your body, lay you bare across this table and fuck you until neither of us can walk straight."

His words, soft as they were, hit her with the force of a volcano. She gaped at him.

"I want to feel your mouth wrapped around my dick. I want...need your hot tongue lapping at my balls, making me come."

Tina swallowed. The spicy tomato zest of her pasta vanished. All she could taste was the salty, musky tang of intimate male skin.

He took a small, uneven breath and then continued. "But not as much as I want to stretch your thighs wide open and bury my face between your legs. Christ, T, I want to lick your pussy until you climax, screaming, in my mouth."

Had Tina's mind been working on full alert, she would have glanced around the restaurant to see if anyone was watching them, listening in. But Gabe's words, his tone and his honesty had her reeling, had her dissolving in a puddle of wanton lust. She too was desperate to strip away her clothes, desperate to lay naked on the table before him.

All she needed now was Connor and their trio would be complete.

"And then..." Gabe closed his eyes and seemed to swallow a moan. "And then, when you're wet and hot and swollen—and still shaking from your orgasm, I want to flip you over, pull your hips up and slide inside you. Deep, deep inside you."

His earlier words echoed through her head. *So goddamned deep inside you I lose myself.*

For long moments he stared into her eyes, not saying another word. He didn't have to. His face was glazed with undisguised hunger.

85

Her heart clanged against her ribs, her stomach tying itself in all sorts of knots. Her arms lay limp on the table, heavy as leaden weights and impossible to move.

"Or," Gabe said at last, and Tina held her breath, "we could just have dessert?"

She had a bowl of gelato. A large, decadent bowl, filled with flavors of Gabe's choice, since she couldn't string a sentence together to order for herself. She ate it without tasting anything, hoping like hell the iced creaminess would cool down her soaring body temperature.

It didn't. Flames roared in her belly, and images danced through her mind. Images of her and Gabe and Connor entwined in the most carnal positions. Gabe, flat on his back, she straddling his hips and Connor behind her. And both of them inside her. Deep, deep inside her.

Tina's cheeks burned. Her breasts tightened, and she drew in a breath that shuddered through her chest.

Gabe took one look at her and leaned in close. Once again he dropped his voice. "I have an erection the size of a frigging cricket bat." He pursed his lips as a muscle ticked in his jaw, and he sat back with a thump. "That's what it feels like anyway."

The thought of his rigid cock had her mouth watering. Tina licked her lips, and then, God help her, she did it again.

"Damn it, T..." Gabe growled at her. "Show me that tongue again and all earlier promises are off."

She abruptly changed the conversation. No way was she going off in that direction. "I need to go through all my pads," she said. "Find the sketches that'll be good enough for the exhibition."

Gabe hesitated just long enough to nod and draw a deep breath. "Your sketches are all good enough to show."

She gave him a half smile. "Nah, they're not. Some are awful." That was enough to head the conversation off into new, safer territory.

"You need some help going through your work?" Gabe asked.

Tina considered his offer. There were at least a hundred pads shoved away in her cupboard. Gabe's strength and assistance would make retrieving them easier. This time her smile was generous. "I'd love some help. Thank you."

Gabe nodded. "Cool. We can start when we get back to your place."

His comment set her heart back into race mode.

Gabe was coming home with her. Back to her place, where all that lay between them and her toys was a defenseless drawer.

"Would you like a drink?" Tina offered.

Gabe sat back and stretched, careful not to knock over any of the sketch pads stacked around the lounge room floor. "I'd kill for a cold one."

She stood. "One beer coming up."

He followed her with his gaze as she walked towards the kitchen. Her jeans pulled around her tight ass, riding low on her hips. Fuck, his dick ached. It had been up and down the whole fucking evening. Mostly up. Willpower, he'd discovered, was not one of his strong suits. Not where Tina was concerned. He was going to have a serious case of blue balls by the end of the night.

He grunted, shifted position to ease the strain on his groin, picked up yet another pad and paged through the sketches. Then regretted it. Shit. Wrong one. Wrong fucking one to choose.

The first drawing was of Connor. He lounged on Tina's bed, his lower body covered by a sheet. A sated, post orgasmic grin was plastered on his mug. Gabe knew the expression well.

He repressed a violent urge to hit something. The only way Tina could have captured that look was to have seen it. Which she had. Altogether too many fucking times.

While Gabe found that sketch perturbing, the next one screwed with his head. This time it was of Connor and him. They both sat on his old couch, butt naked with twin looks of expectation and excitement on their faces. Both had raging boners. Gabe held his hand out in an inviting fashion—summoning Tina over to join them. No question what would happen next.

He saw red.

"Here you go. One ice cold beer."

Too late. He hadn't heard her come back into the room. Now she stood before him, her hand stretched out, offering him a brown bottle. He blinked twice then a third time to clear his vision and looked up at her face. She didn't notice. Her gaze was plastered on the sketch, her cheeks filling with color.

For endless seconds she stared. Just stared. Her eyes turned from almond to dark brown. Her lips parted and her arm began to tremble. Gabe caught the beer just as it slipped from her grip.

Fuck.

He took a long pull on the bottle and then another. Tina continued to stare. The blush in her cheeks blossomed down her neck, and she licked her lips, leaving them red, succulent and glistening.

Fuck, fuck, fuck.

Connor.

Shit, just as things were going so well between the two of them, Connor had to be bought back into the picture. Literally.

"Tina..." he whispered. Christ, what could he say now? How did he wipe Connor out of her mind?

She swiveled around and fled from the room.

Gabe sat frozen, his heart thundering.

Seconds later she was back, her arms full. "Use them," she ordered as she dumped the load in front of him. "Any of them. All of them. Don't care which. Just...use them."

Gabe stared at the cache. While his chest burned with pain, his aching cock stood further at attention. Oh, Jesus. Jesus, fuck. For just a second he saw stars.

He grabbed the vibe closest to him and wrapped his hands around it, imagined fitting it between her legs, slipping it into her wet, hot pussy, and he swallowed.

"Can't do it, T." The words were wrenched from his mouth. "Just not...strong enough." Not when she wanted Connor there with them.

She gawked at him, horrified.

Gabe clenched the vibe tighter, resting the base on the sketch of himself and Connor. "Want you to myself. Won't share you again." He'd have to have steel running through his veins and his heart to share her again.

The horror left her face, replaced by determination—and desire. She cleared her throat. "Make love to me, G."

Gabe ground his teeth together and fought back the impulse to dive on her. He shook his head. "Can't do it, T. Not when you want Connor too."

Her lips curved into a shameless smile. A dangerous smile. Her eyes gleamed with... Oh, fuck, with a carnal thirst. "Then don't move," she whispered. "Not even one inch."

As if he could. His limbs were frozen in despair, his cock hard as the devil.

With that warning, she began to strip away her clothes. Slowly, sensually, one garment at a time. First, she kicked off her shoes and then she pulled her T-shirt over her head. Her singlet followed, leaving her luscious breasts framed in a white lace bra.

Gabe stared, heat washing through his stomach.

She shrugged off her jeans, twisting her hips this way then that to get them down her legs.

He sat motionless, breathless, until her pants hit the floor. Then he dragged in a harsh breath. Not two meters away, Tina stood in her underwear, her tiny thong matching her bra. Through the lace he could see a small, darkened patch—a tiny triangle of trimmed hair.

Oh crap. Shit, fuck and shit again. Never mind blue balls. He was gonna have no balls. They'd explode if she took one more item of clothing off.

She lost her bra.

A hollow cry filled the room, and Gabe realized it was his. This was the ultimate torture, knowing she performed her little act to seduce him, so he could satisfy the lust she had for him—and his best friend.

Her thong landed beside his foot, and she stood butt naked before him.

He closed his eyes and counted to ten, then twenty. He would have counted to a thousand if she let him.

"Open your eyes, Gabe," she demanded. Her voice was closer than expected.

His vision cleared, and he found her right in front of him,

her belly by his face. The smell of her arousal was pungent in the air. Or maybe it was his. Christ knew he was dripping pre-come like a horny teenager.

His mouth opened, his tongue seeking access to the slick folds he knew were hidden between her legs. Holy hell, he was starved for a taste of her.

"Uh uh," she warned. "I told you not to move an inch." Tina leaned over and placed her hand around his. It took a good minute for Gabe to understand her intentions. In his current state of mind, anything other than his jealousy and the all-consuming need to fuck her took way too much logic to comprehend. He loosened his grip, and Tina took the vibe from him.

She stepped away. One pace, two paces, until he could see her whole body, from top to toe. He saw neither top nor toe. He only saw the vibrator that she held between her breasts. Perhaps held was too convenient a word. The vibrator that she tormented him with as she ran it between her tits and then under them. A soft, electric hum began as she ran the toy over her nipples. They tightened into hard beads, goose bumps popping up over the puckered, dusky pink skin.

The vibe was smaller than her rabbit. Thinner too, but the vibrations must have been strong for T to react like she was.

If Gabe were a religious man he would have prayed then and there.

He wasn't, yet he still sent silent words of reverence upwards.

Tina's hand moved downwards.

Gabe ceased breathing.

She widened her stance, just enough so the hand with the vibrator in it slipped between her thighs.

He stared at her, mesmerized, wanting her and despising her. Loving her for being Tina and hating her for wanting Connor.

"Now watch," she whispered, and before his eyes she slid the damn thing into her pussy. The toy glided right in, giving Gabe a good indication of how wet she must be.

Tina moaned out loud, and a massive convulsion wracked Gabe's body. Holy fuck, he was going to come just watching her.

No, he wasn't. If Gabe came, it would be in Tina. Right in the place the vibe was now. Deep, deep in her pussy. And if he came inside her, it would be with a determination to shove every last one of her thoughts about Connor out of her mind.

He fought for control, punching his knuckles onto the carpeted floor over and over.

She writhed before him, rotating her hips in a blatant sexual manner.

Control, goddamn it. He needed control.

He bit down on his cheek hard, drawing blood. Ironically, that was a handy technique Connor had taught him years ago. It worked just well enough to check his premature ejaculation.

"Faster," he ground out.

Tina paused, as if surprised by the intrusion of his voice.

"Move your hand faster," he demanded.

She smiled and moved a little faster, panting.

"Turn the vibe on higher." Crap, his voice sounded like it had been sandpapered.

She obeyed, and her eyes glazed over.

Holy fuck. "Now pull it out."

"Noooo," she objected.

"Take it out, Tina," he ordered.

Slow as she could, she withdrew the toy, pulling it up in front of her hips. It was dripping.

Gabe almost choked on his compulsion to tackle her to the floor and fuck her senseless.

"Don't switch it off," he rasped. "Use it on your clit."

Tina shuddered once, her breasts trembling becomingly. She lurched forward as the vibe made contact with her clit.

"That's it, sweetness. Take all the pleasure you can get from it," he urged.

For long seconds she held the toy in place, twisting it one way and then the other until she gasped. Her shoulders tightened, and her mouth dropped open.

"No!"

She froze.

"Don't come like this." He motioned with his hand. "Slide it back inside your pussy."

She looked at him with eyes blazing. Damn, she was close. Gabe could see what it cost her to hold back. Every muscle was drawn taut. Goose bumps spread over each inch of skin.

Tina slipped the vibe inside her body.

"Now," Gabe said, "Imagine that's me. Imagine that's my dick. Long, hard and dripping for you."

Tina let out a strangled groan.

"What's inside you, T?"

She shook her head.

"What's in your pussy, Tina?" he pressed.

"Y...you are, Gabe," she stammered, and her eyes drew closed.

"How do I feel?"

She moaned. "Good. You feel so very, very...good."

He nodded in grim satisfaction. "Good enough to make you come?"

"God, yes!" The answer exploded from her lips.

Oh, fuck. She was going to give him a heart attack. "Keep me inside you. Don't come yet."

"Wh...when?" She was gasping for air.

"Wait for it..." He tossed the offensive sketch pad aside and yanked off his shirt.

She panted heavily, her hand pushing the vibrator in and out of her pussy. The soft humming floated through the air.

"Wait for it..." Christ, his pants were so tight he couldn't bear it. He undid the button and pulled the zip down.

"Gabe, please," she begged.

"Not yet, T..." Still too fucking tight. His shoes came off, followed by his jeans. He tossed his boxers behind him, and his erection slapped against his belly, the pre-come leaving a damp patch.

"Gabe."

"Touch your clit with your other hand." When she did so with a wild cry, he palmed his erection and squeezed it hard, anything to reduce the need to orgasm.

"Aaawwrrggh. Gabe. P-please."

He nodded to himself. Christ if he didn't give her a break, *he* would explode. "Okay, T. Come for me. Right...now."

Her body gave a violent jerk as she yelled out her release. He watched as wave after wave pulsed through her, rocking her body. Her throaty cries echoed through his ears, pulling at his cock, yanking even harder than before—although he hadn't believed it possible.

He jumped to his feet, took two giant steps and hauled Tina, vibrator and all, into his arms. She was still undulating when he laid her on her bed and climbed on top of her.

She stared up at him with huge brown eyes.

"It's just you and me, T," he said thickly. "No one else. Just the two of us."

She panted as another shudder hit her, vibrating through him.

"Have to have you, T. Have to fuck you."

Tina stopped breathing and then began again, her chest heaving against him.

He kissed her, ravishing her mouth with his. Her lips parted beneath the attack, accepting his tongue into the sweetness of her mouth. Christ, she tasted good. Like wine and woman. She made him heady and high, hot and...hollow. If he didn't get inside of her now, there'd be nothing left of him. He'd fall apart.

Without releasing her lips, he nudged her thighs wide open with his legs and settled himself between them. Of their own accord his hips drew back and shot forward, his dick seeking entrance to her body. He met with a solid barrier and swore to himself. No access. Her pussy was jam-packed full of vibrator.

Gabe drew back with a muttered oath. The interruption brought back a modicum of common sense. He crawled up the bed and reached—once again—for Tina's bedside drawer. As he found what he sought, a hot, wet mouth enveloped the head of his cock and sucked him inside.

Gabe jerked as if he'd been struck by lightning. Burning surges of electricity pulsed through his body, scorching him. "Damn, T..."

Tina made a loud slurping noise as she released him to run

her tongue over his tip, down his shaft, and suck first one ball and then the other into her mouth.

By the time she wrapped her lips around his cock again, Gabe was good and ready to burst. His testicles drew up tight, and pressure built in his dick.

Fuck, he was going come, and it was going to be big. Huge. Four years of waiting was about to result in the biggest fucking orgasm in history.

Or not.

Tina chose that moment to squeeze the base of his dick in a tight fist. So tight that after a couple of seconds the pressure began to subside.

Gabe muttered a hoarse oath of thanks. *When he came it would be inside her.*

He pulled away and sheathed himself with a condom. Tina lay back and watched. She licked her lips and wiped her mouth, then dropped her hand low to manipulate the vibrator.

When she moaned out loud, Gabe knelt between Tina's legs and pulled the vibe out, fast as possible. This time the only thing making her come would be him.

A muted squeak escaped her lips, and her legs trembled.

Goddamn, the thing was soaked with her juices. It smelled like...like sex and like Tina, and God help him, he could hesitate no more. He hauled Tina up so she straddled him, took her mouth once again in a heated kiss and thrust once, hard and fast, so he was buried balls-deep inside her. Deep, deep inside her. Exactly where he'd fixated on being the whole night.

"Oh, Jesus fuck," he growled. "Holy crap, Jesus fuck." Nothing had ever felt so good. Nothing.

His balls pulled tight for the second time, and his spine tingled. *Tingled* for fuck's sake. Tina made him fucking tingle.

And sweat. The sweat beaded on his back and his brow. She felt so damn good, so hot and so wet that all he wanted to do was shoot inside her. Release his load, over and over again, marking her, claiming her, making her his.

Tina's head fell back, her lips parted. "Mmm," she murmured. "Nice."

Gabe saw red. Nice? *Nice?* He was having an out-of-body— out-of-mind—experience, and she thought it was *nice?*

It was all about Connor. Yep, for Tina sex with Gabe was nice. But with Gabe *and* Connor it was perfect.

So much for seeing red. His vision was black now. Dark with lust and jealousy, and God help him, even self-doubt. Alone he wasn't enough for him. She needed more. Needed his fucking best friend.

Bullshit. It was all bullshit. Gabe *was* man enough for her. He was all she needed to reach that ultimate peak, that ultimate orgasm. And he'd prove it to her. Within the next few minutes Tina would forget the word nice even existed in her vocabulary. She'd be using adjectives she'd never dreamed of. He'd show her nice. He'd fucking show her nice 'til she was screaming at the top of her voice, begging Gabe to let her come.

He took advantage of the angle of her neck, leaning in and sucking on the side of her throat. He drew long, patient sips, then short, nipping licks until Tina whimpered. Pausing for breath, he covered the spot with gentle kisses while he drove his dick into her, over and over.

Tina buckled on his hips, bearing down on him, meeting his every thrust with an energetic push of her own. She arched her back, and Gabe leaned in further, pulling a nipple in his mouth. He tugged on it with his lips, abraded it with his teeth and adored it until it was turgid and swollen before turning his attention to the other breast. Not once did he let up on the impetus of his thrusts. Not once did she let him.

Still, Connor sat beside him, an overriding presence in their lovemaking.

"Not enough for her," a voice whispered in his head.

"Yes I am," he roared back in silence and dipped his hand between his body and Tina's. He found her clit and massaged with a feather-light touch.

Tina cried out.

He tormented her nipples with gentle nips and wet licks, drove into her over and over and played with her engorged nub.

When he raised his head, Tina's eyes were closed, her breath coming in uneven huffs and her nipples red and wet from his assault.

"On the count of three, T," he said in a commanding voice.

"One." He thrust and massaged and watched her mouth drop open.

"Two." Another thrust, a strategic stroke of his middle finger, and blood suffused her chest, turning it crimson.

"Three!"

She broke around him, her pussy tightening like a vise, clenching and unclenching as her upper body shot up and slammed into his. She screamed as she threw her arms around his neck and held on for dear life as the orgasm wracked through her.

The urge to come with her was powerful. Powerful enough that every muscle in his body bunched. But the knowledge that she wanted Connor there too was enough to ward off the impetus.

Not yet, he thought. Not until Tina knew for sure that Gabe was the only the man she needed.

With his dick still clenched in her pussy and his hand

caught between their hips, he pressed down on her clit and drew tiny circles around it, sending her into another round of spasms.

"*Gaaaaaabe*," she yelled.

"We're not finished yet."

"M...more?" she gasped.

"Much, much more," he promised and slid out of her. In fluid movements, he turned her around and had her crouch on the bed with her head touching the mattress. He nudged her legs apart to once again kneel between them, crooked his arm under her hips, pulling her butt up, and shoved a pillow beneath her. Then he took a minute to survey his handiwork.

In this position she lay exposed to his greedy gaze. The rounded curves of her ass trembled as small aftershocks shook her body. Her pussy was pink and swollen and shiny with her juices. Gabe leaned in and licked her from her slit to her ass, relishing her taste.

She muttered nonsensically into the sheets.

"Brace yourself, T," he whispered as he took a tube of lubricant and squished a large dollop onto his fingers. The cold glop would come as a shock after the heated assault from his tongue.

Tina jumped as he massaged the lube around her pussy, playing with her folds. She jumped again as he traced the line between her ass cheeks, finding her anus and kneading it with lube.

When he sensed her complete surrender, he dipped one finger into her pussy and one into her ass and nearly passed out when she raised her hips to encourage deeper penetration. He added a finger to each hole, and she ground down against them.

Fuck, was it any wonder he loved the woman? She was so responsive, so open to making love, to experimenting, to...to...well, fuck it, to him.

He didn't need Connor to give her the ultimate satisfaction, and goddamn it, neither did she.

Gently he scissored the two fingers in her ass, stretching her, making room for more. When she twisted, showing her readiness, he withdrew his hand and picked up the vibe. Still massaging her pussy, he rubbed the toy over the crease of her butt, bathing it in the lube and her juices.

She stopped breathing as he positioned it at her anus and pushed against the ring of muscle. Inch by inch, he pressed, giving her time to adapt to the width of the vibe, until it was lodged deep inside her.

"T?" he whispered.

She shivered in response.

"Get up onto your knees. Keep your elbows on the bed." *And Christ, hurry.*

Slowly, languidly, she pushed herself up.

Again Gabe was forced to close his eyes and count to twenty. The vision of her puffy pussy and her toy-stuffed ass sent his blood pressure rocketing.

He opened his eyes to find Tina looking over her shoulder at him. The sultry look on her face pushed his blood pressure higher, but it was the silent request she mouthed that just about killed him.

"Do it now. Fuck me."

Gabe took a long moment to torment her, using the vibe in her ass to fulfill her request. As he pumped it in and out, he leaned forward and placed a finger below her belly, seeking her clit. When he found it, he traced lazy circles around the engorged bud, timing the circles with the pumps.

Again Tina muttered incoherently into the bed.

Gabe turned the vibe onto the lowest setting, careful not to hurt her.

She broke, convulsing on the toy, her ass clenching over and over.

He took the opportunity to ease the ache in his dick, slipping it into her slick pussy and driving it in to the hilt.

Oh shit. He had a minute, tops. No way he was going to last longer than that. God she was tight. Her channel was hot and snug, clamping around his dick, holding him, pulling him in.

"Ga...aa...aaabe!" she yelled. "Yes. Oh, God, yes!"

Not even a minute.

He pulled out and drove back into her, only to be shocked down to his toes when the gentle buzz of the vibrator hummed through the thin layer of skin separating it from his dick. Oh fuck. He could feel it. It drove him insane. Demented him. Jesus, he had to come. Had to...come. Had to...

Again and he again he withdrew and drove back into her, each plunge sending him closer over the edge.

Tina slammed back to meet every thrust, crying out his name, mixing it with God's.

Pressure built, higher, higher, all-consuming, until he could hold on no longer. Tina's wild contractions sent him over. The compulsive clenching of her pussy muscles, pulling at him, tormenting him, brought on his orgasm. With a loud roar he came, spraying over and over again inside her. Luckily voluntary movement was beyond him, because he had a sudden animalistic impulse to tear off the condom and shoot unprotected into her pussy, marking her, staking his claim.

The orgasm kept on and on, yanking rope after rope of come from his balls. Only when Tina collapsed beneath him, still shuddering, did the final pressure of his release end. He jerked as one last shot of semen emptied him.

Moments later, he withdrew from her. Each inch of the extraction was as sensitive as hell. When he removed the vibrator. Tina moaned and sighed.

He tossed the used condom in the bin, set the vibe on the bedside table and collapsed beside her.

No good. She wasn't close enough. He pulled her nearer and wrapped his arms around her. She tucked herself into his chest and gave a soft, contented sigh.

His breath came out ragged and his heart raced. "I love you," he whispered as he ran a hand through her silky hair.

Tina's only response was a soft snore.

Chapter Seven

She stared at him in morbid fascination. "You want me to wear that?"

His brown eyes shone with lust. "Uh huh."

"To the restaurant?"

He nodded in affirmation and held his hand out.

She swallowed but took his gift, holding it in her palm. With a soft buzz it whirred to life, vibrating against her skin, tickling her.

Gabe grinned. "Remote control."

Her pussy clenched—in response to both the toy and his smile. She raised an eyebrow. "And who gets to hold the remote while we're at dinner?"

He winked. "I do."

That was all the information she needed. She spun around and headed to the bathroom, emerging minutes later feeling decadent and naughty. Pressed against her clit and held in place with thong-like straps was a tiny butterfly.

Gabe's surprise return visit seven weeks ago had turned into a regular Sunday-night event. At some point, the Sunday visits stretched out to incorporate Wednesday evenings as well. And then, interestingly enough, Friday nights too. They didn't always go out. Sometimes they just stayed in and watched TV or chatted or pashed on the couch.

It had been seven weeks of wondrous lovemaking and enchanting reawakenings. She hadn't had sex like this in four long years. Not since her last encounter with Gabe. Or, to be more specific, with Gabe and Connor.

"Are you wearing it?" Gabe asked now, his voice devilish and sexy.

"Yes."

"How does it feel?"

She thought about it for a second, imagined the purple vibe pressed against her clit, and said in all innocence, "Soft. Comfortable. Cozy."

He growled and shoved his hand in his pocket.

Tina jumped.

"How about now?"

The butterfly vibrated with a soft, stimulating buzz. Not hard enough to make her come, but strong enough to shock her into a heady state of arousal. Moisture pooled between her legs, and her heart beat a little faster. She closed her eyes and sighed with pleasure.

"How does it feel now, T?" Gabe asked again.

She turned her head towards the sound of his voice and searched for his mouth. She found his lips and treated herself to a long, dreamy kiss. "It makes me feel like spending the evening at home," she whispered on a sigh.

Gabe pulled away and dipped his hand back into his pocket. The soft humming ceased. He smiled at her, his eyes dancing with mischief. "Not a chance. You and I are going to dinner."

Tina spent said dinner in a state of persistent excitement. While Gabe gave the impression this was just another evening out, she knew from his dark eyes and high color he was as aware of the butterfly as she was. He turned the damn thing on at strategic and inappropriate moments. As the maitre d' showed them to their table, he dipped his hand in his pocket. She almost tripped as sensation flooded her pussy. It was off by the time they were seated. When the waiter came to take their order the toy began to buzz again. Tina requested her food in a high-pitched voice, and Gabe partook in a longer-than-normal discussion about the merits of red wine versus white with the waiter.

This wasn't the first time Gabe had suggested she wear a toy out. Last Friday evening he'd searched her drawer and found a small butt plug. She'd sat through two hours in a movie with the damn thing wedged inside her. Gabe had not looked at the screen. He'd spent the entire time watching her squirm, a wicked smirk playing on his mouth. Her front door was closed maybe a minute after returning home before she was naked and on the carpet. Gabe made love to her with the toy still inserted in her ass. She came three times before he lost control.

Tina rested her elbows on the table and her chin in her hands as Gabe chatted to the waiter. She closed her eyes, relishing the tantalizing secret they shared. In the noise of the restaurant she couldn't hear the butterfly at work, although its effects were clear.

The toy shut down.

"The waiter's gone," Gabe said in a low voice.

She wrinkled her nose. "Pity."

He responded with a deep chuckle.

"Mmmm," she murmured. "If the butterfly was a little wetter and a little warmer, I could pretend it was your tongue."

The soft humming started up again. "If it were my tongue," Gabe murmured back, "you'd be convulsing in your seat."

She ground her butt on the chair, trying to increase the pressure of the toy against her pussy. "I'm almost there."

The vibrations stopped. She growled her discontent. He winked.

They started up again when she took her first bite of food.

"I thought the salmon would taste better like this," Gabe told her.

"It might," she answered. "But when you tease me like that I'm not even aware of what's in my mouth."

Gabe watched her with a satisfied smile. His gaze was warm, his posture relaxed. They spoke the whole way through their meal. They discussed the exhibition, which would open next Sunday night, and Tina's anxiety about it. By the time they'd exhausted the subject, Tina felt less apprehensive, in part because Gabe had promised to hold her hand the entire time—if she needed him to.

They chatted a little about their food, a little about Tina's sodden underwear, and a lot about the everyday events that had taken place since the last time they'd talked on the phone, which was less than twenty-four hours ago. Gabe had taken to calling her last thing at night, every night. She relished the calls, looked forward to discussing her day with him and savored his daily updates.

As they waited for their coffees to arrive, Gabe clicked the switch to on once again, and she sank back in her chair with a breathless sigh. Damn, it felt good—tiny streaks of pleasure flying through her nerves. She was happy. As happy as she'd been four years ago with Gabe and Connor. Maybe even happier, she admitted as desire trickled through her.

"What are you thinking?" Gabe interrupted her reverie.

She answered without hesitation. "How right tonight feels. How good it is to be with you."

The buzzing stopped. He leaned forward, his gaze intense. "I'm thinking the same thing."

Her body was on fire, the gentle stimulation of the toy and the enticing company of the giant opposite her arousing her to new heights. She almost hoped he didn't turn the butterfly on again. She wasn't sure she could resist temptation much longer. The continual teasing had driven her past common sense. She wanted to make love to Gabe. Now. Before she came without him.

Her breasts tightened, the nipples pulling into hard beads. "It's time to leave," she said. "Let's ditch the coffee. I have a sudden urge to be alone with you." To share her happiness and end this perfect evening with a perfect climax. Together. Just the two of them. "What do you—"

"Shit." He cut her off with the sharp oath. "Connor!"

"Um, huh?" Nope, Connor had not featured in her musings at all. In fact he hadn't featured in her thoughts for a very long time.

Gabe stood, all signs of his contentment evaporating.

"Connor," he said again and this time followed the name up with, "Maddie."

It was only when a couple approached the table that Tina realized he was greeting them.

Oh, dear God.

Her hand began to shake. Blood drained from her face. Connor was here. *Connor.* The other half of Gabe and Connor.

She struggled to catch her breath as she looked up at the face of the man she'd loved so dearly. The man she'd loved as much as Gabe. He was still every bit as beautiful as he had been back then. His blond hair brushed over his neck and collar, while his chiseled features were offset by his unshaven beard and moustache. Lord, oh Lord, he looked good enough to eat.

Connor clapped Gabe on the back then turned his attention to her as Gabe gave Maddie a hug.

"T." Connor looked at her with his usual dazzling smile. "Nice to see you." He walked round the table, leaned forward and kissed her cheek.

The instant his lips touched her skin Tina jumped. She gawked at Gabe, horrified, as the soft, insistent buzz started up again.

Gabe stared back at her, expressionless.

The silent interchange lasted no more than a few seconds, but it left Tina both unsettled and horny. She blinked and turned back to Connor. "Hey, C," she said and wished her voice sounded at least halfway normal.

"How are you doing, beautiful?" Connor asked, the use of the endearment as casual as the use of her nickname.

She nodded foolishly, hyperaware of the soft hum of the butterfly. "I'm good. You?" Good? She was stunned stupid. Gabe was here, Connor was here—with his girlfriend—and there was a butterfly vibrator flapping against her clit.

"I'm good too. Better than good." He held out his hand, and the other woman took it in hers. She was a voluptuous beauty. "T, this is Maddie. Maddie, this is Tina."

Maddie's smile was warm. "It's nice to meet you. I've heard a lot about you."

Tina's eyes widened. "You have?"

Maddie nodded. "Gabe speaks about you often." Then she added with a twinkle in her eye. "Only positive things."

Tina looked in his direction and was met with the same disconcerting blank stare as before. She eyed him in despair, begging him in silence to switch the damn toy off.

It buzzed on.

"I've heard good things about you too." She turned back to Maddie. "I believe you're the one who tamed Connor." Oh, God, this was hell. It was bad enough seeing Connor again. But did she have to meet his lover at the same time? And did Gabe have to play with her pussy while everything else was going on around her?

Maddie looked at Connor. Connor looked at Maddie. They smiled at each other. "I do my best," Maddie said.

"We've just ordered coffee," Gabe said. The muscles in his jaw seemed tense, as if they were locked in place. "Why not join us?"

What? Was the man out of his mind? Hard as she tried she could not think of a more uncomfortable situation. Already the tension was unbearable.

"What do you think?" Connor asked Maddie.

"Sure," she agreed.

Wonderful. Maybe we can discuss the merits of group sex. Or perhaps Maddie and I can debate which of the two men had a bigger dick, Gabe or Connor. If anyone was in a position to argue the point, it was Maddie.

Tina cringed in her seat and then wished she hadn't. The movement forced her clit closer to the vibe, causing all sorts of reactions in her pussy.

She tossed a beseeching look at Gabe and almost did a double take. He stared back at her with eyes as bleak as a cloudy winter night.

"What is it?" she mouthed.

And that quickly his expression was blank again, the emptiness in his face as solid as a brick wall between them. He made no attempt to answer her.

She blinked, stunned by the silent interchange.

Tina forced herself to make polite conversation with Maddie and Connor, although all she really wanted to do was haul Gabe into a quiet corner and find out what the hell was wrong with him.

"Did you get the invitation to my exhibition?" she asked Connor.

"I did." He nodded.

"We're looking forward to it," Maddie said.

She'd felt obliged to invite them. It was only fair, seeing as Connor featured in a few of the sketches she, Valerie and Gabe had chosen to display. "You're coming?" she asked, surprised, and then regretted the choice of word as the butterfly fluttered on. If she wasn't mistaken, the vibrations were a little stronger than before. She scowled at Gabe. Last thing on earth she needed was to have a blinding orgasm at the table.

"Of course we are." Connor smiled. "We wouldn't miss it."

"That's nice to hear." God, her voice sounded all squeaky. She took a sip of coffee and cleared her throat. "You might see a familiar face or two in some of the sketches," she warned.

"Mine?" Connor asked with a grin.

"And Gabe's," Tina supplied, determined to ignore the tantalizing hum beneath the tablecloth.

"Cool. Maybe I can buy one of the sketches of me for Maddie."

Yep. Sure. That's exactly what Maddie would want on her wall. A drawing of her lover—sketched by his ex-lover. The woman was destined to love it.

Not.

Tina wracked her brain for something to say after that, but

damn it, conversation was almost impossible. Sweet pulses of pleasure were shooting through her, Gabe sat opposite her, staring, his expression switching from bleak to empty—until he looked at Connor or Maddie. Then he was all smiles and good conversation.

Connor sat beside her as if nothing was wrong. As if her world wasn't turned upside down and inside out by the whole disconcerting scenario. And his girlfriend sat discussing where she might hang the sketch.

Argh.

"I've heard you're moving back to Sydney," she said to Connor as she thanked God she'd remembered how to make small talk.

"Moved," he clarified. "Yesterday."

"Well, welcome home." She tried to smile, but it felt forced and unnatural. "Have you found a place to live?"

Oh, sweet Lord, the persistent vibrations were making her even wetter.

"He has. He's staying with me," Maddie said, and Connor reached across the table to clasp her hand in his.

Tina's heart lurched. Connor was in love, no question about it. He was as smitten with Maddie as she was with him.

Gabe said nothing.

Before Gabe's silence and the awkwardness of the situation overwhelmed her, she drained her coffee and stood. "I'm off to the ladies' room." She excused herself and beat a hasty retreat to the back of the restaurant.

If she'd expected Gabe to turn off the butterfly as she walked away, she was disappointed. The toy whirred away as she waited for the occupied bathroom to open. It seemed to last an eternity, but finally the room was free, and Tina rushed in.

She was about to close the door when someone forced it open again. Gabe crowded into the small room behind her and locked them in.

"What are you doing?" she asked him, knowing she shouldn't be surprised by anything he did anymore.

Gabe didn't answer. His eyes were dark, his face closed.

God, he looked so miserable. "Are you okay? What's the matter?" What had happened to the smiling, laughing, charming Gabe? Where had he gone?

He ignored her questions, "Are you still turned on?" he asked in a gruff voice.

"You know I am," she gasped. She was close to breaking point, and having Gabe so near in such a confined space was not helping matters.

He stepped forward. "Do you want me to help you?"

She swayed towards him, craving his touch. "I want you to turn the darn thing off," she murmured. "Especially with Connor and his girlfriend sitting right there."

"Does it make you hot?" His voiced dropped, so low it almost sounded menacing. "Seeing Connor again?"

Tina's mouth dropped open. "What?"

"Are you wet for him, T?"

She stared at him. She *was* wet. And hot—and, damn it, Gabe knew it.

"Gabe," she said on a moan. "Please..."

"Please what?" His mouth twisted in a grimace. "Please turn it off? Or please help you?"

"We're in a toilet, in a restaurant," Tina pointed out, almost at the end of her tether. "Please, just turn it off."

Gabe hooked an arm around her waist and pulled her

close. "You're not being honest with me or with yourself." His tone was hard, unforgiving, and it made her stomach clench with doubt and insecurity. This was not the Gabe she knew.

She almost forgot that thought a second later when his hand made its way under the hem of her dress and crept up the inside of her thigh.

Tina groaned and dropped her head against his chest, inhaling his familiar scent, relishing it. Oh, God, his fingers were by her pussy, pushing her panties aside and resting on the butterfly, pressing it against her. "Touch me," she croaked, barely able to breathe. "Please, touch me."

"You mean like this?" He dipped a finger lower and ran it over her slit.

She bucked against him. God, that felt good. Her body leapt to attention, just like it always did when she came into contact with Gabe.

"Fuck," he swore. "You're dripping."

Tina shivered. Gabe seemed...pissed off. She clutched the collar of his shirt with both hands and looked up at him. "Gabe, w-what's the matter?"

A muscle ticked in his jaw, yet he said nothing, choosing instead to slide his finger deep inside her pussy.

"Oh, my God," she breathed as powerful sensations radiated through her limbs.

He added another finger, pumping them in and out.

"*Aaahhhh.*" Tina couldn't speak. Couldn't think. She clutched his shirt tighter, pulling his head down so she could kiss him, needing to feel his tongue in her mouth, his lips against hers. Needing the intimacy and the reassurance Gabe could give her.

He turned his face away from her, added another finger

and continued to fuck her. Hurt and rejection mingled with a cutting relief. The whole evening she'd been on edge, horny, desperate for an orgasm. Now it was minutes away, seconds. But damn it, she didn't want to come like this. Not with Gabe's rebuff stinging her heart.

"Gabe, please," she begged, looking for both reassurance and relief.

He twisted his fingers and pushed in again. "How does this feel?"

"Good." Because it did. So good she almost lost it. "And terrible." As much as she needed her orgasm, she didn't want it like this. Not when Gabe seemed so angry.

He turned to her and whispered in her ear. "Can anyone else make you this hot?"

Chills ran down her spine. "No one has ever made me feel this way." Like she could explode and cry at the same time.

"So, it's just me?" He slipped his other hand beneath her skirt and rolled his fingers between her ass cheeks.

"God, yes," she cried, not sure whether she was responding to his touch or his question.

"I'm the only one who makes you feel so good?" He stroked in and out of her pussy.

She squeezed her muscles around him. "Y...yes."

"Say it." Still with the stroking, still with his hand on her ass.

"Say...what?"

"Say I'm the only one." He pumped a little faster.

She teetered on the edge of her orgasm. "Y-you're the only one." Without a doubt.

"Then come for me, Tina." His voice echoed with grim satisfaction. "And call out *my* name as you do."

He curved his fingers and pumped into her a little faster. At the same time he stroked her anus. The combined fuel of the butterfly and his actions tipped her over the edge. She came hard, breaking on his hand.

She cried out his name, searching again for his mouth, but it wasn't there. Her release stretched out longer than she would have liked, the result of an evening spent on the verge of orgasm.

"Say it again," Gabe whispered as she convulsed. "Say my name."

"Gabe." Speech was close to impossible. "*Gabe,*" she breathed as the last few spasms wracked their way through her groin. She collapsed against his solid body, using his strength to hold herself up.

The butterfly whirred to a stop, and Gabe removed his hands. His breath was an uneven rasp in her ear, and his erection pressed into her belly.

For just a moment he took her weight, letting her rest against him. His breath blew threw her hair. And then he stepped away.

Tina stumbled.

He steadied her but came no closer. She grabbed onto the basin and leaned over it, her breath coming a million miles an hour.

With a light tap, he placed the remote control on the countertop. Then he paused, motionless, before sighing deeply.

"Tina..." There was so much uncertainty in his voice she turned to look at him.

He shook his head, frowned, and then as though he couldn't help himself, pressed the gentlest of kisses to her neck. Just one kiss. One beautiful kiss that whipped her breath from her body and was over way too soon.

Long before she gained even the slightest semblance of control, the lock clicked, the door swung open behind her, letting in a draft of air, and then it was closed.

Tina found herself alone in the small bathroom, shaking. That last, exquisite sensation of his lips on her neck had seemed frighteningly like a kiss goodbye.

Chapter Eight

"He won't be here?" She looked at Valerie in despair.

"I'm sorry." Valerie shrugged, looking helpless. "No."

Everyone who mattered in Tina's life would be attending tonight's opening. Her family, her friends, her colleagues. Her boss was coming with his wife and three adult daughters. Her hairdresser told her she was bringing her new boyfriend along. Even Connor and Maddie would be there.

The only person who had chosen not to grace her with his presence was the one she wanted beside her most of all. The one who had made this all possible. The one who had promised to hold her hand through the scary bits of the evening.

"Yet he came to the gallery this morning for a private viewing?" she asked again, desperate for some understanding, some insight into Gabe's absconding from her life. Why would he need a private viewing anyway? He'd helped her select every sketch displayed. He knew each of them almost as well as she did.

Valerie nodded. "At eight-thirty sharp. And trust me, my dear, I don't get out of bed for just anyone so early on a Sunday morning."

"Did he say why he couldn't make it?" Oh, God, she was beginning to sound pathetic. But she hadn't heard from him in over a week, and she was getting desperate.

"No." Valerie raised an eyebrow. "Perhaps you might ask him yourself?" Then she frowned, looking thoughtful. "But I will say this. Gabriel is a large man. A mountain. And yet..." Her voice trailed off.

"And yet what?" Tina prompted, almost afraid to hear the rest of Valerie's sentiments.

"And yet this morning he seemed...small. As if he'd lost inches off his height overnight."

Tina slumped back in her chair. She could identify all too well. She herself felt all of three feet high. As if holding her head up and her shoulders back was too difficult. Damn it all, it was Gabe's fault. How dare he walk away from her again? What was he thinking? He'd spent an entire evening seducing her, getting her excited, and then he'd had the audacity to act disappointed when he'd discovered she was aroused. Disappointed enough to leave her.

She gritted her teeth. She'd spent the last week puzzling over Gabe's behavior, Gabe's absence, and now she was getting pissed off. *Of course* she'd been turned on. She'd had a freaking vibrator clamped over her clit for three hours. What the hell else had he expected? He'd been working the goddamned remote control—

"Tina, are you okay?" Valerie peered at her. "You look as if you're about to burst a blood vessel."

She took a deep, calming breath. Just as well Gabe wasn't going to show his ugly mug at her exhibition tonight. Attacking him with a knife in public would not make for good publicity.

"I'm fine," she assured the gallery owner. "Just nervous about the showing."

He deserved a freaking knife. How dare he stampede back into her life like he had, make her fall in love with him all over again, and then vanish?

Valerie patted her hand. "You'll be fine. Better than fine. By tomorrow this time, you'll be famous. The talk of Sydney. Every discerning art collector in the city will be clamoring to purchase a Tina Jenkins original."

Tina smiled at Valerie. She might be bossy, opinionated and over the top, but Tina had come to adore her. "Thank you again for doing this. This is an opportunity of a lifetime."

Valerie brushed off her gratitude. "I'm only doing it because you're going to make me a lot of money. It's Gabriel you owe your thanks to." Before Tina had a chance to respond, Valerie stood and shuffled her out of the office. "And now I have to meet the caterers and ensure everything is set up for your debut." She air-kissed Tina's cheeks. "Go make yourself beautiful for tonight. I will see you later."

Dumped by Gabe and tossed out by Valerie. Just great. Tina felt about as wanted as swine flu. She went home to sulk.

When she arrived there however, she was diverted from her undertaking. Sitting on the front steps leading up to her building were Connor and Maddie.

She stared at them, incredulous. "It's like stepping into a caricature of my life. Everything's familiar, yet nothing is right."

Connor grinned and patted the step beside him. "Sit, T," he invited. "We just came by to say hello. That's all."

She eyed him with suspicion. Oh no. No way. Not eight weeks ago she'd gone down this exact road with Gabe. He'd also just stopped by to *say hello*. Then he'd proceeded to sweep her off her feet. Look where that had gotten her? *Nowhere.* She was as miserable now as she had been four years ago. No way was she going that route with Connor.

"I am not going to sleep with you," she told him before turning to face Maddie. "Or you for that matter." She turned back to Connor and folded her arms. "We tried it once. It didn't

119

work. I'm not exploring the scenario again."

Connor let out a full-bellied guffaw while Maddie stifled a laugh.

"That's not why we're here," Connor assured her when he stopped chuckling.

"Oh." Tina had the grace to blush. "Ah. So, uh, why are you here?"

"To discuss Gabe," Connor said.

Tina flashed him her sweetest smile. "Oh, lovely. Let's chat, shall we? Maybe then you can pry my fingernails off with a screwdriver. It should be just as much fun."

Maddie gave her a sympathetic look, and Tina found herself warming to the other woman. Awkward circumstances aside, Maddie seemed nice.

Belatedly, Tina took Connor up on his invitation and sat on the step beside him with a sigh. "Okay," she said, this time without sarcasm. "Let's talk about Gabe."

"He's miserable," Connor told her.

"Good," Tina answered. So was she. And she was miserable because of Gabe, so she was glad he was miserable too.

"He looks a little like you do," Connor said.

Tina raised an eyebrow. "Short and blonde?"

He gave her a quick grin. "No. Unhappy, dejected and pissed off."

Tina studied her shoes. "Why are you telling me this, C?"

"Because I haven't seen Gabe like this in a long time, and it worries me."

She grimaced. "He's a big boy. He can look after himself."

"He's crazy about you, Tina," Maddie said. "Head over heels, madly in love with you."

"Yeah?" She pictured herself frantically seeking Gabe's mouth as he fucked her with his fingers, craving his kiss, his love, his affection—and finding nothing but his cold rejection. She gave Maddie a dubious look. "Well, he sure has a funny way of showing it."

"Cut him some slack, 'T,'" Connor said. "You know that talking things out isn't one of Gabe's strengths."

Tina looked at him, pretty sure he had no clue just how deeply Gabe's rejection had cut her. "Yes, I'm well aware of that. But not one word in over a week is perhaps taking his *weakness* a little too far, don't you think?"

"I think he's hurting," Maddie said.

Good. She bit her lip.

"I think you're hurting too," Maddie added, all too insightfully for Tina's peace of mind. "Would you like to talk about it?"

Tina couldn't hold back her dubious look. Maddie, the current lover of her ex-boyfriend and the ex-lover of her current boyfriend—well, current up until a week ago, anyway—was offering her a friendly ear.

Maddie smiled. "Yeah, I know. It's weird. You and me talking like this, pretending to be friends, when, well..." She motioned to Connor and then to herself, then included Tina in her gestures. "When, you know, we hardly know each other, yet have all this shared history. It's a little odd."

Tina snorted. "A little?"

"Okay," Maddie snorted back. "A lot."

"I'll just give you ladies some space on this one." Connor shifted up a step.

Maddie caught her eye and grinned. Tina grinned back and found herself liking Maddie even more. Under different circumstances she suspected the two of them might have made great friends.

"Did something happen between the two of you?" Maddie asked. "You looked so happy together when we saw you at the restaurant last week, and then, minutes after we joined you, that all seemed to change."

Tina should have found Maddie's question a little too...brazen, but she didn't. It was difficult to take offense to her in any way. She sighed. "We were getting on well, and then we weren't," she agreed. "The only thing that changed was that you joined us."

Maddie said nothing, just let Tina's response hang between them.

"His entire demeanor was different after that." Tina thought out loud. Gabe had turned from an attentive, sexy date to a sad, aloof, cold stranger. "It was like seeing you switched a button in his personality."

From there her mind wandered to the only logical conclusion she could think of—and God help her, she wished it hadn't. She hated the conclusion. Despised it. "He's in love with you, isn't he?" she asked Maddie.

Maddie's jaw dropped.

Tina began to tremble. "You know," she said, clasping her hands in her lap and listening to her heart break in two, "he said he was okay with you and Connor being together. He seemed so cool about the whole situation, and I believed him." She'd been wrong. Gabe was far from cool. He was all twisted up inside, and she'd only noticed when Connor and Maddie had interrupted their meal. But then that was the first time she could have noticed. It was the first time she'd seen them together. "He told me he'd given you his blessing," she said to Connor, hoping he couldn't see the utter desolation that was tearing her apart. "He even said he was happy for you guys." She'd taken his words at face value. What an idiot he must think her. "He must have lied to protect you both from his real feelings."

Connor made a strange, choking sound, before wheezing out a baffled, "What are you talking about?"

"Oh, C, it all makes sense now, don't you see? How could Gabe pretend to be interested in me when the real owner of his heart was nearby?" Damn it, why was the revelation so difficult to accept? Why did it make her chest clench in agony and her throat close up in grief?

Connor looked at her in disbelief. "You know, if I wasn't so fond of you, I'd attempt to beat some sense into you."

Tina grabbed his thigh—the closest of his body parts—and gave it a comforting squeeze. "I'm sorry, C. Shit, this must be awful for you too. Knowing you and Gabe are both in love with the same woman."

He rolled his eyes. "If Gabe loved Maddie he'd be with her right now. He'd never have made the same mistake twice. He let you go. He wouldn't have let Maddie go."

"But he did," Tina argued. "He did it for you."

"Gabe's a good guy. The best I know. But he's not a saint. He gave Maddie and me his blessing because he wanted you, not her."

Christ, Tina wished that were true. Wished with all her heart. But she couldn't bring herself to believe it. Not after the way Gabe had behaved in that bathroom.

"Tina," Maddie said, "I can assure you Gabe has no romantic feelings towards me. He never has. What we shared was sex. End of story."

It might be the end of the story for Maddie, but the thought of Gabe having sex with another woman—a woman he loved—made Tina want to throw up.

Maddie must have noticed her distress. "The only woman he's loved in the past four years is you."

Tina shook her head. "Then why would he have gotten so angry when you arrived at the restaurant?"

Maddie bit her lip. "I don't think it was my arrival that angered him." She shifted her gaze to Connor.

Tina frowned. "You think it was Connor's?" *Huh?* "Why would Gabe be upset about seeing his best friend?"

Maddie said nothing. She tilted her head and looked at Tina's hand where it rested on Connor's thigh.

Tina looked at her hand too. Then she looked at the leg beneath her hand and got distracted. Oh, dear Lord, her hand was on Connor's leg! Connor—her ex-lover.

She stared at her hand, dazed, waiting for sparks of electricity to shoot through her, burning her palm where it clasped his thigh.

Nothing happened.

She waited a little longer.

Still nothing.

She shifted around and switched hands.

Nothing. She was gripping Connor's leg and she felt...nothing. Nothing! No increased heart rate, no tug of arousal, no difficulty breathing. Not even a tiny leap in her belly.

Connor sat without saying a word.

She peered up at his face, searching the features she'd always found so endearing. When her gaze settled on his beautiful blue eyes she almost gasped out loud.

She felt nothing.

And yet when Gabe touched her, looked at her...

"Oh, good grief!" How could she not have grasped the truth before? How could she have been so blind as to not see what was so obvious now?

"T?" Connor's eyes narrowed in concern. "You okay?"

She didn't answer, just kept staring as reality barreled through her.

"T?" Connor said again.

"I don't love you," Tina told him.

Connor looked somewhat taken aback.

"I never did," she said, knocked sideways by the fact.

He gave her an uncertain smile. "It doesn't happen often, but right now, I'm not sure what to say."

"Don't say anything," the sage Maddie offered. "Just let Tina talk."

Tina offered him a shy smile. "I'm sorry. I know that sounds terrible, but I'm just realizing..." Oops. Maybe this was too much information.

"Realizing what, T?"

It wasn't fair to dump all this on Connor. She needed to sort it out in her own head first.

When she didn't answer him, Connor said to her, "T, I've seen you buck naked, on your knees, making love to me and Gabe at the same time. You think it might be a little late for inhibitions? Just say what you need to say."

"Connor!" Tina blushed scarlet and looked at Maddie, mortified.

Maddie rushed in to reassure her. "Don't worry. He's pretty much seen me the same way. Just say it. Whatever it is, he can take it."

Tina couldn't help but smile at her. "No wonder Gabe and Connor love you. You're cool."

Maddie frowned. "Gabe doesn't love me."

"And Tina doesn't love me." Connor said, steering the conversation back to her incredulous discovery.

"I don't," she agreed. "I never did."

"So, what are you only just realizing?" Connor prompted her.

"That it was Gabe all along."

"What was?"

"He was the one I loved. Not you. I just couldn't see it then. I couldn't separate the two of you." She smacked her forehead. "God, how could I have been so blind? How could I not have comprehended this years ago?"

"If it helps, I was blinded by them both as well," Maddie confessed. "It took me a while to work out Connor was the one, not Gabe."

"But they're so...so different."

"Yeah," Maddie agreed, "but together they make quite a team."

"It was the teamwork that did it. That's what confused me." Tina turned to stare at Connor as if seeing him for the first time. In a way, she was. She was seeing him through clear eyes, eyes no longer tinted by the misconception of love. Sure, he was gorgeous, but still... "I don't love you," she told him, still befuddled by her comprehension. "You just had me thinking I did because you were so darned good in bed."

"He is good, isn't he?" Maddie concurred.

"Yeah, and with Gabe, well the two of them..."

"I know." Maddie nodded. "Believe me, I know."

"But it's not just about sex, is it?" Tina asked Maddie.

"It's about love."

"And without love, the sex isn't enough."

Maddie gazed at Connor. "But with love..."

Tina dropped her head in her hands. With love everything was different.

Which explained why sex with Connor had gone from good to stupendous when Gabe entered the picture. It had nothing to do with Connor and everything to do with Gabe.

No wonder she and Connor couldn't make it alone after Gabe had left. The magic hadn't been with Connor, it had been with Gabe.

And no bloody wonder it had taken all of a couple of hours of seeing Gabe again before she'd tumbled, ass first, into bed with him. She still loved him. She'd never stopped.

Sweet Heaven. She loved Gabe. Only Gabe. No one else but Gabe. She'd fallen head over heels in love with him the minute Connor introduced them.

"I love Gabe," she told Connor and Maddie. "I do."

Connor gave her an encouraging nod. "That's good. Very good. But maybe you should tell him this?"

"Maybe I should," Tina concurred, keen to seek Gabe out and share her wondrous revelation with him.

Then her heart sank. Gabe had walked away from her. Why on earth would he want to hear she loved him? "Or maybe not," she said listlessly. "Doesn't really matter what I feel about him. Gabe doesn't feel the same. Not after Friday night."

"Oh, for God's sake, you still don't get it, do you?" Maddie asked, raising her voice for the first time. "Gabe feels the same way. The reason his behavior changed on Friday night was because Connor sat down next to you. He thinks you're in love with his best friend—and it's killing him."

Gabe slumped on his couch in the darkened living room. The blinds were drawn and the lights turned off. Sound blared from the TV, but Gabe had no idea what program was on.

His gut hurt something rotten, and the glow from the screen stung his eyes. He considered switching the TV off but couldn't be bothered. It required too much effort.

He stared at the unopened bottle of Absolut Vodka on the table in front of him. He should open it and have a sip. Have a glass. Have the whole fucking bottle. He should get pissed on the stuff. But he couldn't be bothered. Too much effort.

He halfheartedly thought of phoning through for some home delivery. Maybe Thai. Maybe pizza. In the end he couldn't be bothered. Too much effort.

And when the bell rang he even rallied with the idea of opening the door but didn't. Too much fucking effort.

He was through making an effort. He was through bothering. He'd spent two months pouring his heart into making an effort with Tina, and look where that had got him.

Absofuckinglutely nowhere.

She'd taken one look at Connor and her eyes had blazed with the same desire Gabe had begun to believe she'd reserved just for him.

How fucking wrong could he have been? How fucking stupid? Yep, he did believe Tina loved him. Just like she had before. As half of a whole. Half of Connor and Gabe. And watching her watching Connor just verified that for him.

Alone, Gabe still wasn't man enough for her.

The bell rang again and again. Whoever stood outside was one persistent fucker. Still, persistence wasn't enough to get Gabe's ass off the couch. Perhaps if he'd been more of a man, like Tina needed, he would have made it to the door.

Fuck.

Gabe dropped his head back and closed his eyes. After a time the ringing stopped. Maybe the hurting would stop too. Nah. Probably not. If it hadn't quit for four years, it sure wouldn't quit now.

With that agonizing thought, Gabe willed himself to sleep. At least the oblivion of unconsciousness would be more tolerable than the continual obsession about the woman he loved and his failure to please her.

A flood of icy water hit his face, shocking him awake.

"What the fuck?" he gasped as he scrambled to his feet.

Cold droplets splattered down his nose and onto his chest, wetting whatever parts of his shirt hadn't been soaked in the initial onslaught.

"*That* was for refusing to kiss me on Friday night," a biting female voice informed him.

"*This* is for walking away from me. *Again*." Another icy shower hit him, this time from behind, drenching his hair, neck and shoulders. He swung around to face his attacker, opened his mouth to yell and was met with a third frigid blast of water. He swallowed at least half of it, choking in the process.

"That one is for even thinking about not showing up to hold my hand on the most important night of my life."

A blast of wind tore through the room, doubling Gabe's sodden discomfort.

"And this one—" yet another torrent of liquid hit him, "—is just because you pissed me off."

She nodded with grim satisfaction, walked onto the balcony—through a door that Gabe had not remembered leaving open—switched the tap off and wound the hosepipe back into place. Demurely she told him, "It's cold out here. I'd hate for you to get sick." Then she pulled the blind down, slid the door closed behind her—and vanished.

What the fuck?

Gabe shook his head as if to clear the cobwebs, although fuck knew whatever cobwebs had been there should have been atomized in the deluge.

How had she gotten into his flat? The front door was locked. He knew because his keys were still in the door where he'd put them this morning. And for that matter, how the hell had she left his flat?

Christ, she hadn't left. She was on the balcony...

No, she wasn't. She was gone.

Cold and wet, Gabe stood on the small ledge outside his living room, dumbfounded. Where the hell had the little spitfire disappeared to? He peered over the railing and down two floors.

No way. No fucking way had she climbed over. Not to get down and not to climb up here either. She would have killed herself in the process.

Well then, where the hell was she?

Gabe yanked his shirt off and wiped his face with it. He charged inside and headed to his front door, using the shirt to dry his hair. Not that it helped. He tossed it on the floor.

He pulled the handle, swore when nothing happened, took a second to turn the key and stormed out into the hallway. Shit, what if she *had* scaled the goddamned balcony? He wouldn't put it past her. He wouldn't put anything past her.

Fear edged down his spine, and he took off at a sprint, heading for the stairs.

He came to a careening halt not five paces later.

Tina stood at the open front door of his neighbor's unit, smiling at its occupant.

"No worries," the divorced father of two was saying. "Glad to have been of assistance."

Tina shook his hand, thanked him again and turned to leave. At which point Gabe, seeing red, grabbed her waist and threw her over his shoulder.

She let out an outraged shriek.

He marched back to his place.

"You two have a pleasant afternoon," the neighbor called after them with a chortle.

"Put me down, you big oaf," Tina demanded, pounding his back. "You're...making me...wet."

Gabe slammed his front door, stormed over to the couch and dumped Tina on the now soaked cushion. And not a second too soon, since she'd begun attacking with her feet, and had she connected, his ability to father children might well have been compromised.

"You have two seconds to explain," he snarled at her.

"Ah, so *now* you want to talk," she said with her trademark sarcasm.

"I don't want to talk," he corrected. "I want answers."

"You've given me the silent treatment the whole week, but now you want answers, I have to be forthcoming? Go fuck yourself, Gabe."

He grimaced and resisted the urge to either kiss her stupid

or smack the wall. "How did you get into my flat?"

She gave him one of her sweet smiles. So sweet he could not doubt the insincerity of it. "Your charming neighbor, Colin, let me in."

"Colin has no way of getting into my place." He set her straight.

"Sure he does." Still with the sweet smile. "Why he's just a hop, skip and a jump over your balcony."

He gawked at her. "You went through Colin's flat to get to mine?"

"Well, Carter, you sure as hell weren't letting me in voluntarily."

He rubbed his eyes. "That was you banging on my door?"

She folded her arms over her breasts and treated him to a stony silence.

Gabe sat in the chair opposite her, his heart performing a hundred-meter sprint in his chest. "What are you doing here?" he asked in his calmest voice.

Christ, she looked incredible. Her lips were painted cherry red and her eyelids smoky blue. They matched the navy dress that ended an inch above her knees and offered just the slightest hint of cleavage. A large, silky scarf-type thingy was wrapped around her shoulders, warding off the cold.

She eyed him evilly and then smiled again. Her sweet, sarcastic smile. "I came here to chat about Connor."

It took a lot to bring a man of Gabe's size to his knees, but with just that one sentence, Tina succeeded.

Her smile vanished. "I thought I might give you a chance to explain why you acted like a complete moron the second Connor and Maggie showed up the other night."

The hair on the back of his neck stood on end. Once again

he pictured the look on Tina's face as she spied his friend for the first time in four years. The glazed lust in her eyes, the rounded "oh" of her mouth and the way her chest rose and fell in pre-orgasmic flutters.

Suddenly Gabe was cold. Freezing. And fucking wet too.

"Her name is Maddie," he told her. "As in Madeline. M.A.D.D.I.E. *Maddie.*" And with that he stormed to his bedroom, ripping his jeans off as he went. The damp denim stuck to his skin, making a slurping sound as it came off. "And she's Connor's girlfriend," he yelled. "The woman he loves. The only fucking woman he loves."

He kicked off the jeans and threw open his cupboard doors, staring blindly at his clothes. Jesus, he wanted to hurt someone. Wanted to rip someone's fucking throat out. But whose? Whose fucking fault was it that Tina loved Connor as much as she did him? Connor's? Tina's? His? Where did he lay the fucking blame?

He jumped when an arm wound itself around his waist and a warm hand touched his stomach.

"And you are the only man I love," Tina said behind him as she rested her head against his back.

Gabe stilled. Even his lungs ceased working for a moment.

She tightened her hold on him. "I love you, Gabe," she said, whispering the words against his spine, shooting chills up his neck.

Christ, he wanted to believe her. So much. But he couldn't. Not after he'd seen her response to Connor in the restaurant.

She pressed light kisses to his back. "I have since the day Connor introduced us. I loved you while I was with Connor, and I loved you when you left." Her voice dropped. "You hurt me, but I loved you still."

Her hand trailed a feathery path up his chest, and his groin responded. Fuck, his heart was a fucking tangled knot of pain, and she could still make him hard with just a touch.

"I've never stopped. It's you, Gabe. Only you. You are the only man I love. The only man I ever could."

"Yep, just me...and Connor." It was Gabe's turn for a little sarcasm. "The only men you could ever love."

Her head moved against his back, as though she were shaking it. "Nope, not Connor. Never Connor. It was you all along. I just couldn't see it. I couldn't separate you two out, and I didn't want to. Because that would have meant the man I'd lost my heart to rejected me. Walked away from me." She took a shuddery breath and released it, the air a gentle wisp over his buttocks. "It would have hurt too much to acknowledge."

"Damn it, Tina, I saw your face. I watched your reaction when you saw him again." Shit, he sounded like a lovesick, jealous fool.

Perhaps that's because he *was* a lovesick jealous fool.

"What did you see, Gabe?"

Fuck, again he had to picture it. Fuck, fuck, fuck. "Your eyes." He closed his own against the agony of the memory. "The open lust in them. The naked desire in your face."

She sighed. "Did you ever stop and think that maybe all that lust and desire had nothing to do with Connor?"

He snorted in disgust. "So who was it for? Maggie?"

"Maddie," she corrected with a soft laugh and then made him jump again. The hand that was not caressing his stomach dipped into his undies. The sensitive flesh on his dick screamed to life as the lightest vibration buzzed against it.

"Oh, damn." He gasped. "T..."

The buzzing ceased.

"Three hours, Carter. I endured this for three hours on Friday night." The vibrations started up again, and he drew in a burning mouthful of oxygen. "I had to sit with you in public and pretend—for three hours—that I did not want to drag you home and fuck you into oblivion."

Silence. Stillness. Nothing but the rasping sound of Gabe's own breathing.

Until the soft hum filled the air again, messing with his head.

"You tormented me the whole evening, Gabe." She moved her hand, positioning the butterfly on the base of his cock.

The light flutter drove him nuts. Drove his nuts nuts. Fuck, it wasn't enough. He wanted her hand wrapped around his dick. Her mouth... Her pussy...

"Who do you think my open lust and naked desire was directed towards?" Stillness once again. "Connor? Maddie? Or maybe it was the waiter?"

She pulled away then, and Gabe was left colder than before without the heat of her body to warm him.

Oh, Christ, was it possible he'd read the whole situation wrong? Could that look have been for him and not Connor? That dazed gaze of naked lust and adoration? For him?

Jesus fuck, maybe it could have.

Maybe, just maybe, she did love him after all. Just him. Not Connor.

"T..." He turned around, grappling with the thought. God knew he wanted it to be true. He wanted her to love him. Just him. No one else.

She sat on the edge of the bed, staring at him. Her gaze was ice cold.

What the...?

"T," he said again, but she cut him off.

"You treated me like a stranger in that bathroom."

He froze, the accuracy of the accusation blasting through him. He'd tried so hard not to think about it, not to remember his terrible behavior, but of course he'd failed outright.

"You're right." He nodded. "I acted like a jerk, and I apologize. I was jealous," he added hoarsely. "So fucking jealous it hurt."

"And pushing me away helped ease that pain?" Her eyes flashed.

"Nothing eased that pain." He pressed his fist against his eyes. Christ, just thinking of the night made him see red. "I had to show you that Connor meant nothing to you. That it's me you love. Just me."

"By bringing me to orgasm in a public bathroom? Without throwing me even a crumb of affection in the process? That was the best way you could show me?"

"God, I'm sorry."

"You turned away from me. You shoved your fingers in my pussy, yet refused to kiss me." Her neck flushed red. "You rejected me while you fucked me. And then you left!"

"I read your response all wrong. I thought you...wanted Connor. Christ, I hated how wet you were. How excited you'd been to see him. I had to prove I was the only one who could make you come." He grimaced.

"It had nothing to do with Connor, Gabe. I was wet for you."

"I didn't know that." He fell to his knees in front of her. "The last time we discussed Connor you told me you couldn't separate us out. You said you loved us as two halves of a whole." He dropped his forehead on her knees. "The first time we made love, this time round, it happened after you'd seen your sketch of me and Connor. It killed me. Knowing you wanted me only because you'd seen him. But I couldn't say no. I wanted you too damn much."

"Oh, Gabe." She sighed and ran her fingers through his hair, sending tingles racing across his scalp.

For sure she was the only woman who could make him tingle.

"It had nothing to do with Connor," she said. "It was all you. You'd spent the whole day and night seducing me. You introduced me to Valerie, you made me laugh, you wined and dined me. And you told me in no uncertain terms that you wanted to fuck me. I was oblivious to the sketch of Connor. It was the sketch of you, G. I saw it and I wanted you, more than I'd ever wanted you before." She laughed. "Which is almost impossible seeing as how badly I wanted you before."

"How badly you wanted Connor and me before," he corrected.

She tugged on his hair, pulling his head up until he looked at her.

"See, G, that's where I was wrong. All along. It was never about Connor. I never loved him. But when I met you... Everything changed. I fell head over heels. I convinced myself I loved both of you because I was with both of you. But when you weren't there anymore there was nothing left between Connor and me. There couldn't be. I loved you, not him." She shook her head. "It's just taken me four years to admit that to myself."

"What are you saying, T?" He needed her to spell it out. To tell him in one syllable words he'd be sure to understand. To comprehend. To believe.

"That I love you, G. Just you. Not your friend. You."

The last ounce of doubt melted away. "You do, don't you."

"God, yes!"

"Even after I walked away from you on Friday night?"

Her eyes darkened. "I hated that. But yes, I still love you."

He took her hand in his, brought it to his lips and kissed her knuckles. "I love you too."

She wrinkled her nose. "What about Maddie?"

Huh? "What about her?"

"Do you love her too?"

He frowned. "No. I never did. I told you that weeks ago."

She blushed. "I just had to make sure." Then she shot him a look of pure mischief. "Well then, how about Maggie?"

He snorted. "I don't love her either."

"Good."

He smiled then, a smile borne of relief and of love. Four years it had taken to reach this point. Four very long, very lonely years. "It's just you, T. I only love you."

She smiled right back and made a show of tossing the butterfly vibe over his shoulder. "Then prove it. Make love to me. No toys, no aids, just you. Show me you are the only man I'll ever need in my life."

Gabe loved using toys with Tina. Dug it. He loved how responsive she was to the added stimulation, how keen she was to play and explore. But for the last eight weeks the compulsive need he'd felt to use the toys went beyond Tina's enjoyment. He'd used them to make up for Connor's absence. He'd used them to prove she didn't need another man in his bed. He was man enough for her.

And now he could prove it to her—without the toys. He was all the man she would ever need again.

"With pleasure," he growled, and had her naked and flat on

her back in less than a minute. And when he pressed his lips to hers, he knew for sure she was his. Tina surrendered to him, offering the most delicious kiss he'd ever tasted. So delicious he refused to release her mouth. While her tongue played with his, he found her breasts with his hand and caressed them until she moaned against his lips. He kissed her as his finger found the slick folds of her pussy and the plump bead of her clit and teased her until she broke on his hand.

He swallowed her cries as he stroked the sensitive bud between her butt cheeks, making her come again, and he kissed her as she pumped his rock hard dick with her bewitching fingers.

He pulled away long enough to lose his undies and don a condom, and then he was back, taking her mouth, slipping his tongue between her lips and settling between her legs to claim her.

Inch by glorious inch he pressed into her, relishing the satiny smoothness of her tight channel, the creamy moisture that eased his way until he was encased in the velvety heat of her body.

Still he kissed her, tasted her, consumed her. They moved together as one, her hips rising to meet his thrusts, rhythmically, sensuously, his lips gliding over hers, melding to hers.

It didn't matter how many times before Gabe had made love to Tina. This, now, was different. This time she made love to him too. It wasn't about sex, or fucking, or breaking records for the number of orgasms induced. This was love, and dear God, it was perfect.

Gabe didn't try to hold back. He couldn't. When Tina's rocking changed, when it became frenetic and frantic, Gabe let go. He gave in to the urgency of her demands and drove into her over and over again. As her muscles began to contract around him, his balls pulled tight against the base of his dick. When she cried out as she arched her back, Gabe lost control.

They came together, she convulsing beneath him in wild abandon, he shooting his release into her once, twice, a hundred times.

God, his orgasm seemed to go on forever, a rapturous, wondrous liberation of emotion. And with every jerky ejaculation inside her, she spasmed again, the two of them spurring each other on, until they collapsed in a tangled heap on the sheets.

"Tina," he gasped when he could drag air into his lungs. "Damn, T, that was..." he shook his head in awe. "That was... Just damn."

"Nope, Gabe," Tina answered, just as breathless, "that was love. Pure and simple."

A smile blossomed on his face. That was exactly what this was. Love. Pure and simple.

No question about it.

Going All In

Dedication

With special thanks to Viv Arend and Valerie Tibbs, whose sharp eyes, wise comments and wonderful friendship help more than they could know.

Jennifer Miller—your unfailing guidance and advice make me a better writer. Thank you for taking a chance on this book.

And my boys—you know I love you.

Chapter One

"I call, and I raise you twenty dollars." Julia Savage placed her bet. The evening was drawing to a close, and she figured she might as well take a bit of a chance before leaving Jay Baxter's flat.

Jay gave her a look that scorched all the way through to her toes. "Raising the stakes, are we?" He checked his cards and winked, stirring up every dirty fantasy she'd ever had about him—and she'd had her fair share. "Cool. I see your twenty."

Hunter Miles laid down his hand. Serious as ever, he shook his head, making his blond hair glisten like wheat under the lights. "Too rich for me. I fold."

Julia resisted the overwhelming urge to run her hand through his silky locks. She nodded at Hunter instead, making sure her expression was blank. "Okay, Jay. Deal the turn."

Jay burned a card then flipped one. Queen of Hearts.

This time Julia let a smile play on the corner of her mouth. Sometimes a little bluff went a long way in a game of poker. Real life, on the other hand, was a different story. "I bet another ten." She added more chips to the growing pile in the center of the table.

Jay grinned and matched her bet.

Her heart lurched. "River card?"

"At your command." Jay looked at her a second too long, then burned another card and showed her the river.

It took a moment to comprehend what the card was. Her brain couldn't compute much besides the men on either side of her. They left her mind reeling and her heart thumping.

Ten of Spades.

Hunter whistled, his lips pulling into a sexy pout, and Julia made sure her gaze stayed on the cards. No point in examining his delectable mouth now. She had to focus on her game.

Two tens, a queen, a jack and a nine lay on the table.

Julia narrowed her eyes then opened them wide. She held a lousy Three of Hearts and Six of Diamonds. In other words— nothing. "Thirty dollars."

Jay looked at her with a frown. Then he looked some more, after which he glanced at his cards one last time. "Pot's yours," he conceded with his charming Jay smile and laid down his hand.

Julia gave a satisfied nod, handed in her cards and helped herself to the winnings. She suppressed the snicker that fought for release. She'd played them both like a pro. No way would she show them her piddly hand. Bluffing was her forte and damned if she wasn't good at it.

Heck, she'd been bluffing them both for months, pretending her interest in the two men ran no further than their weekly Friday-night poker games. Pretending she wasn't head-over-heels in love with both of them, and she didn't lie awake at night wondering which one would make a better boyfriend or lover.

God knew she wanted one as a boyfriend or lover. The question was, *who would she choose?*

Damn it, she couldn't answer. That was her whole problem.

She wanted them both equally. There was no way she could opt for Jay over Hunter, or Hunter over Jay. Not if being with one man meant never having the other.

The guys had no clue how often she dreamed of them or how each dream drove her insane with its lack of clarity. She'd see herself making love with one of them, and then midvision, that man would morph into the other. Hunter would become Jay, or Jay would become Hunter.

It was odd that she couldn't separate them in her dreams, because the men were so different in real life. Jay was a loveable clown, and Hunter an earnest, focused go-getter.

Her affection for Jay had crept up on her over the last year or so. Like her, Jay was a pharmaceutical rep. They worked the same territory, Sydney's Eastern Suburbs, and had made it a habit to meet up often for lunch. Over salads and sandwiches he'd regale her with stories of doctor calls, keeping her in stitches of laughter. It was Jay who'd invited her—the only woman ever—to join his poker club after he'd learned about her passion for the game. Which was where she'd met Hunter, a product manager from another pharmaceutical company. She'd taken one look at the solemn, intense blond hunk and lost her heart to him too.

Julia glanced at her watch. Eleven-forty-five. The rest of their poker club had gone home already, leaving just the three of them.

Hunter took the pack and shuffled. "Up for another round?"

"Always," Jay answered.

"You bet," Julia chimed in. "But last one for me." It was a good idea to leave before the night got too late. Before the idea of propositioning one of them became too appealing to refuse.

Jay poured her another glass of red wine and topped up his

and Hunter's scotch. "Should we up the stakes?"

Julia scowled at him, determined to hide the fact that the very idea sent shivers of desire racing up her spine. "Shit, Jay. How many times do I have to say it? I'm not playing strip poker."

Jay grinned, once again sending flames shooting through her belly. "Chill, Jules. I'm talking about opening bets. Fifty bucks too high for you?"

God, the man was insufferable. Tall, smug, funny, gorgeous, sexy and way too confident for his own good. Julia would give her right arm to sleep with him.

"Make it sixty," she dared.

Hunter gave a low chuckle. "You've got style, Jules. I'll give you that."

"You in then, Blondie?" She shot him a challenging look, and her heart skipped a beat. Men didn't come much better looking than Hunter. With his square jaw, bottomless brown eyes and straight nose, he epitomized handsome. She'd give her left arm to sleep with him.

Hunter *harrumphed.* "So much for having style." He counted out a pile of chips and pushed them forward. "I'm in, Four Eyes."

It was Julia's turn to *harrumph* at the nickname, but she didn't. Hunter had been calling her Four Eyes for so long, she knew it was his affectionate way of referring to her. She simply pushed her glasses up on her nose and chanted, "'They say men don't make passes at girls who wear glasses. But do girls who wear glasses make passes at men?'"

His smoldering gaze made her toes curl. "Don't know about other men," he said, "but this girl's never made a pass at me."

Damn the man. He was too sexy for his own good. And she

would have made a pass at him months ago—when she'd met him at her first poker game—if she hadn't had such strong feelings about Jay.

"Me neither." Jay stared at her speculatively, his beautiful blue eyes sparkling with humor. "Think that's because she's not interested, or because she wears glasses?"

Oh, she was interested all right. How could she not be? Jay could make her heart sing as easily as he could bring a smile to her face. And Hunter's eyes seemed to see more than she ever showed him. His serious nature inspired soul-deep conversations. She adored talking to him, adored comparing their views of the world and discovering his opinions weren't so different from hers. Heck she adored him. Which brought her back to her original problem—how could she choose one guy over the other?

Damn it! Why couldn't she just be in love with one of them? It would make life so simple.

"There's only one way to find out if she's interested," Hunter said. "Lose the specs, Four Eyes."

When would she learn to keep her mouth shut? They'd take any opportunity to tease her mercilessly. She shoved forward sixty dollars' worth of chips. "Deal the cards, Blondie."

Jay added his bet to the pile. "It's cool, mate," he reassured Hunter. "Let her wear the glasses 'til the hand's been played. She can't see a thing without them."

Again Hunter flashed his smoldering look. "It's a deal. One more round...and then all bets are off." He doled out the cards.

"You boys are full of it," Julia told them as she inspected her hand. King and Ace of Spades. "There's so much hot air in this room, I'm surprised the glasses in question haven't fogged up yet." She took a sip of wine to moisten her dry mouth. The three of them fooled around like this often, and the lighthearted

147

banter, heavy with sexual undertones, got to Julia every time.

It was Jay who answered as he picked up his hand. "They will fog up," he said, "just not from hot air."

The corner of Hunter's mouth twitched, but he didn't give in to a full-blown smile as he dealt the flop. A four, a king and an ace.

Julia's heart jumped into her throat—and it had nothing to do with the cards in front of her.

They all checked.

She tapped her glasses. "Still clear as crystal," she observed.

Hunter flipped a seven.

Jay grinned at her and bet twenty dollars. She and Hunter matched the bet.

Hunter flipped the river. Another ace.

Jay bet thirty.

Julia went all in.

Hunter paused for a moment. "Things are heating up," he said to his cards. "Get ready for the fog, Four Eyes." He pushed all his chips into the center of the table. "I call your bet."

Julia raised an eyebrow.

Jay folded. "Want me to get you a serviette?" he offered her. "To wipe off the glasses?"

"I'm good, thanks." She grinned at him then looked at Hunter. "What are you holding?"

"Read 'em and weep." Hunter showed his hand with smug look. A pair of kings. "Full house." He leaned forward to gather the chips together.

"*Not* so fast, Blondie." She laid out her cards. "Another full house. Ace high."

Hunter stared in astonishment.

Julia turned to Jay. "Better give Hunter that serviette. It looks like he's going to cry." She polished off her wine. "And on that note, gentlemen, I believe I will take my leave. With my glasses still on and clear as crystal."

"It's because she can't see well enough without them to drive home," Hunter told Jay knowingly.

"Take them off, Jules." Jay winked at her. "You can spend the night here."

Julia's stomach did a three-point turn. "And where will I sleep?" She eyed the couch dubiously.

"Spend the night with me, Four Eyes. You won't sleep at all." Hunter's voice was a little lower than usual, and its timbre caught her between the legs and tugged.

Julia studiously ignored him. She packed away the cards and counted her chips, hoping her hand wasn't shaking hard enough to knock everything over. "Two hundred and seventy dollars." She smiled a haughty smile. Her highest winnings to date.

"Keep it. I won't charge you for staying over," Jay told her, deliberately misunderstanding.

"Cash 'em in please, Blondie. I need to get home."

Jay threw his arms up in surrender. "Fine. This week you get to leave. Don't count on it next Friday." Before she could respond, he stood. "I'm going to make some coffee. Want some?"

"Love some," Hunter said at the same time Julia refused. She had to go, before temptation overwhelmed her. The only thing stopping her from doing something dumb, like tackling one of the guys to the floor and throwing herself on top of him—naked—was her inability to choose which one she'd tackle.

Jay went into the kitchen, and Hunter walked over to Julia.

He offered her the money, and she accepted it, keeping her arm stiff to hide her trembling. Before she could pull away, Hunter caught her hand in his.

"Take off the glasses, Jules." This time there was not a hint of a smile playing on the corner of his mouth.

Julia looked at him, startled. Her heart began to beat in an irregular pattern.

He ran a thumb over the back of her hand, sending streaks of delight whizzing up her arm. "Take them off," he said again, his voice a mere whisper.

"Hunter..."

He took the money and placed it on the table. Then he leaned over until his mouth was close to hers. "You said it, sweetheart. Men don't make passes at girls who wear glasses." His brown eyes narrowed to tiny slits.

She gaped at him. Quick comebacks had always been her strong point. So why, in the face of Hunter's physical proximity, did she struggle to put together the simplest of sentences? Never mind coherent speech, why did she struggle to breathe?

His gaze was on her lips now. "Okay," he conceded huskily, "maybe they do." With that, he closed the space between her mouth and his.

Julia would have gasped out loud, but her lips—and her voice—were possessed by Hunter. His lips weaved their magic across hers, nibbling, stroking, caressing.

Her breath hitched in her throat. Oh, Lord. She'd spent months lusting after him, months fantasizing about him, and now Hunter was finally kissing her.

With a soft groan, he touched the tip of his tongue to her lips. Her mouth drew open as if by will of its own. Her acceptance of his silent appeal was all he needed. Hunter took control of the kiss with an expertise that wiped thought from her mind. All she could focus on were the exquisite sensations he evoked within. The warmth that suffused her body, the tingles that raced over her skin and the shivers that crept up her spine.

Sweet heaven, the man could kiss. Not that she'd expected anything less, but melting on a chair in Jay's dining room was a most startling turn of events. One she'd craved for four months. One she'd only dreamed would transpire.

Hunter pulled away, inhaled and licked his lips. "Mmm. You taste as decadent as the wine you've been drinking." He licked his lips again.

With his tongue engendering all sorts of wicked thoughts, Julia didn't stop to think about her answer. She'd wanted him to kiss her since that first poker game. Since she'd looked at him and stars had exploded. "You taste like sex."

With a groan he crushed his mouth to hers, kissing her with an ardor that made her pussy clench. Her dreams had never been this good—in her fantasies his lips had never been as thorough. Lord, he only need say the word and she'd strip naked for him.

But then, Jay need only say the word, and she'd strip naked for him too.

The thought of the brown-haired hunk in the kitchen brought a whimper to her throat. Hunter's kiss was exquisite. Out-of-this-world amazing. But how could she kiss him back knowing she loved Jay too?

How could she not?

A rush of heat pooled between her legs. Her nipples tightened into hard beads. Damn! *The man could kiss.*

Without releasing her mouth, Hunter pulled her up and backed her across the room. Blinded by passion, she tagged along, her trust in him absolute. Besides, she wasn't about to end the kiss just so she could see where he led her.

When her back touched the wall, he sighed and crowded into her, pressing his body against hers. Every inch of him was hard, from his muscular thighs to his powerful arms. From the solid wall of his chest down to the thick erection in his jeans.

"Miles," a voice sounded behind Hunter. A low male voice that made her shiver.

God. Jay was here. Watching her with Hunter.

"Go 'way, Baxter," Hunter mumbled against her lips.

"Not on your life," Jay said. "I want me a taste of that."

He did?

Hunter resumed the kiss, his mouth filling hers with delicious promises.

"Shift over, Blondie," Jay said with quiet determination.

What the...? That hadn't sounded like the chilled-out, laid-back Jay at all.

Hunter sighed and began to pull away. His lips clung to hers as his tongue gave a final sweep of her mouth. He pressed his rigid cock against her groin before taking a deep breath and stepping aside.

She didn't have time to protest. Jay took Hunter's place before she registered the loss of contact with him. He gave her a dazzling smile and claimed her mouth in another bone-melting kiss.

Jay. The guy who tempted her on a weekly basis with his shameless flirting but never quite carried through on his half promises, was now brushing her lips with his, teasing her with his tongue and igniting all sorts of fires in her belly.

Kissing him was nothing like kissing Hunter. While his lips and tongue tantalized, his body caressed, moving first this way then that, ensuring every part of her was stroked by every part of him. He was just as solid as Hunter—everywhere—but his height and her position threw Julia off balance. His hands spanned the width of her back and waist, and she stood on tiptoes, wrapped her arms around his neck and held on for dear life, never wanting to let go.

The kiss they shared wasn't just temperature-raising, toe-curling unbelievable, it was a culmination of a year's worth of teasing.

As horny as it made her—and man, was she ever horny—Julia wasn't sure she was ready for this. How could she kiss Jay *and* Hunter? She'd spent months agonizing over her love for both of them. Months trying to choose one over the other—and now they were both kissing her.

On the other hand she wasn't sure she was ready to pull away. Because no one had ever kissed her quite like Hunter *or* Jay. No one had ever evoked such a physical response from her in quite so short a time. In fact, no man had ever kissed her two seconds after another man had pulled away.

Jay lifted his head, catching his breath. God, she was kissing Hunter and Jay. *Both of them!*

Too much. It was happening too fast. She couldn't let it go any further.

Could she?

Lordy, if she felt this good being kissed by two men, imagine how she'd feel making love to them both.

What the fuck? Was she out of her mind even considering the idea?

Her answer was a resounding yes. She had to be out of her mind. Good girls did not do that sort of thing, and she'd been raised to be a good girl.

Even as her mouth opened to welcome back Jay's tongue, she used her hands to push him away. He let her go—but didn't release her lips.

Hunter took her hand and twirled her out of Jay's embrace, back into his own arms. Jay swore. The world spun out of control. Her chest hummed, her pussy clenched and she accepted Hunter's greedy kiss again. For a second. A minute. An hour.

Then there was pressure at her back, another person melding his body to hers. His hips cradled the top of her butt, and his cock pressed firm against her lower spine. Her hair was pushed to the side, and feather-light kisses were pressed to her neck. Tiny nips attacked her ears, so light the sting was less like pain and more like darts of pleasure rushing through her.

Here she was, cocooned between the two finest-looking men she'd ever had the pleasure of meeting, being treated to a sensory seduction of lips and tongues, and damned if she wasn't steaming past boiling point.

Why the heck did good girls not indulge in activities like this? It felt incredible.

If she didn't put a stop to this, fast, there was no question where they would end up. And much as she fancied herself in love with both men, she couldn't quite see herself sleeping with them at the same time. Sure, ménages were okay in erotic romance books, but in real life? Not even close.

Although God knew the thought of a three-way with Hunter and Jay had her perspiring. It had her heart smacking against her ribs so hard she feared it might cause permanent damage. And damn it, it had her knickers so wet the evidence might well show through her jeans.

With more reluctance than she would have liked, she drew away from Hunter's kiss. "Stop," she whispered. "Please."

Her breasts ached, and her stomach rolled with rebellious anger. Her head might be telling her one thing, but her body spoke a very different language.

Brown eyes stared intently at her. The same brown eyes that seemed to look into her soul whenever they talked. "You sure that's what you want?" Hunter asked.

Jay's lips trailed delicious sparks down the back of her neck, making her shiver.

"N-no. I'm not at all sure," she admitted, and was rewarded with a hand skimming the side of her breast. She closed her eyes as extreme pleasure fluttered through her chest. Whose touch it was, she couldn't fathom. Either of them would have set off the same reaction. "But I can't do this. It...it's not right."

"It's...different, perhaps," Jay said. "But it's as right as you want it to be." He nipped her earlobe one final time, and then he too stepped aside, freeing Julia from her exquisite prison.

She moved away from the men, her steps shaky and uncertain. How could two men seducing her, together, be right? Even if she did love them both?

Because it feels incredible, her body answered, still talking a different language from her head.

Yes, her head agreed. *It felt bloody fantastic.* But still, two men? At the same time. Uh-uh. She couldn't do it.

Without saying a word, she grabbed her denim jacket and car keys and walked to the front door. She knew she'd left her winnings but couldn't face going back for them.

"Four Eyes?" Hunter stopped her. She turned to face him. His bottomless brown eyes brimmed with desire. "It's not true," he told her, while Jay opened the door, making it clear he wouldn't prevent her from leaving. "Men don't give a shit whether girls wear glasses."

Chapter Two

"I cannot believe it."

Julia cringed.

"Both of them?" Kim stared at her, perplexed.

"Don't look at me like that. It was just a kiss." Yeah, and the pope was *just* a priest.

"*A* kiss?" Her sister raised her eyebrow.

"Okay, a few kisses." Julia studied her nails. "Is that so terrible?" God, she hoped no one could hear their conversation. The coffee shop they sat in was small, and other customers need only prick up their ears to listen in on them.

Kim set her cappuccino down on the saucer. "I don't know. Is it?"

"Shit," Julia bit out in frustration. "You're supposed to be helping me out, not questioning me. Give me some big-sisterly advice."

Kim looked at her apologetically. "I'm sorry. You just, er, surprised me."

"Yeah, well Jay and Hunter surprised me." There was the understatement of the century.

Damn, she'd spent four months with the men, teasing and flirting. What had changed? Why had Hunter suddenly upped the stakes? What had inspired him to kiss her?

What if he'd never touched her? Would Jay have shown her his hand? Would he have taken the initiative and kissed her? And if he had, would Hunter have pushed him out of the way to lay his wager, like Jay had?

Did it matter? The cards had been dealt. Both Hunter and Jay had expressed their interest. The rules had changed. The game was different. The only question Julia was left with was did she still want to play?

"Please, help me," she begged her sister. "Tell me what to do about it."

"Hmmm..." Kim thought out loud. "Have you spoken to them since Friday?"

"I'm kind of doing my best to avoid them." No way could she face either of them yet. "Jay phoned a few times to meet for lunch, but I made up excuses so I wouldn't have to see him." The last time he'd phoned, she'd stammered out some garbage about not being able to take time off work for lunch and still keep up her call rate, what with Christmas just around the corner.

"You can run, Jules," Jay had told her with a husky laugh, "but you can't hide." He'd hung up, leaving Julia shaken and aroused.

"How about Hunter?" Kim asked.

Julia's skin grew hot at the very mention of his name. "He's phoned too." Which was out of character for him. "But I was too chicken to answer his calls, so I texted back saying I'd see him at poker tonight."

"Brave of you," Kim said sarcastically.

"Hey, you kiss two men you have the hots for, at the same time, and then let's talk about brave."

"Russell might protest," Kim pointed out.

Julia pulled a face. "See, you're lucky. Being married and all, you don't have to worry about these things."

Kim frowned. "Even when I wasn't married I never found myself in a situation like this."

"I didn't tell you about Friday night so you could get all righteous with me," Julia snapped. "I've never been in a situation like this either. I thought you might be able to offer some sage advice."

Kim laughed. "You're talking to the Queen of Conservative here. Why on earth do you think I'd have any wise words of wisdom?"

Julia eyed her with an evil grin. "Because you're weren't always the Queen of Conservatism, Miss I-slept-with-three-different-guys-in-one-week Savage."

Kim grinned right back. "Yeah, so maybe I did. But not at the same time."

Julia sniffed. "I haven't slept with Jay and Hunter at the same time."

"Yet."

"You're not helping," Julia grumbled.

Kim sat up straight and wiped the smile off her face. "Okay, let's talk this out logically. You were nuts about them before this all happened. How do you feel about them now?"

Julia blinked. How could she tell her sister that she'd spent the week in a sexual frenzy, desperate for the touch of both men? She'd been so aroused by Jay and Hunter's advances that she'd spent every night since with her faithful vibrator. And damn it, more than once she'd found herself wondering what it would be like using two vibrators at the same time.

Although the toy had helped to soothe the ache in her pussy, its benefits had been temporary. A jellied penis didn't kiss her or hold her afterwards. Nor did it ease the bewildering ache in her heart. She wanted Jay and Hunter for that. Jay *or* Hunter.

"I'm still nuts about them," was her candid response.

"Both of them?" Kim asked. "Or now are you more attracted to one than the other?"

Julia shook her head in despair. "Both of them. I still can't choose." If anything, the interlude had just reinforced her feelings. "And yes, before you say anything else, I am considering sleeping with both of them."

Kim's eyes widened, but to her credit she didn't make any further sarcastic remarks. "Here's what worries me." She hesitated as though wondering how to word her concerns. "I think that if you take this any further, the three of you will never be able to go back to being what you were before, or to having what you had. If you sleep with both of them the dynamics of your friendships change. They have to. There's now sex involved."

Julia's stomach sank. That was not what she wanted to hear.

Her thoughts must have been reflected on her face because Kim hurried on. "Look, I know you've got this vision of yourself being involved with one of them. But do you think that either Jay or Hunter would want a relationship with someone who slept with him *and* his friend?"

Julia blanched. "I hadn't thought so far in advance." Since last Friday she hadn't thought further than lusting after both of them and knowing she shouldn't. Served her right for asking Kim's advice. She wanted a serving of reality, and her sister was giving her just that.

Kim squeezed her arm. "I'm sorry, Jules. I know I'm not saying what you want to hear. And remember, I haven't met either guy, so I may be wrong." She shrugged. "But I don't know any man who would be okay with that scenario."

Julia thought about it. Would either Jay or Hunter consider having a one-on-one relationship with her if she did sleep with both of them?

She didn't have a clue.

"Okay, let me turn the scenario around," Kim said. "Let's say you sleep with both of them, and then you introduce them to Mom and Dad as your...boyfriends. How would you feel?"

"Are you out of your freaking mind?" Julia exploded. Almost immediately she lowered her voice to a whisper as people at the tables around them turned to look at her. "I could *never* introduce them to Mom and Dad under those circumstances!" God, the mere thought was excruciating. Her parents would be appalled.

"Why not?"

"I'd be embarrassed. Downright mortified." As open-minded as her folks were about issues like sex before marriage and spending the night at a boyfriend's place, they were also open about their expectations of their daughters. Neither Kim nor Julia had been under any doubt growing up that they were expected to get married and have children. Kim had already lived up to her responsibility. She had a husband and a gorgeous daughter. Now all eyes were turned to Julia as the family waited for her to announce her nuptials to some lucky bloke.

Julia had made it clear she wasn't ready for marriage. One day, but not now. Still, that didn't mean her parents would welcome two men into Julia's life, and certainly not at the same time. On the contrary, they would be horrified.

Kim nodded and cringed, and Julia knew she understood exactly how she'd feel. "Does that tell you anything?" her sister asked.

Julia closed her eyes. "Mom and Dad wouldn't approve."

"Afraid not."

Julia took it a step further. "And if I'd be all embarrassed about introducing them, it probably means I don't approve either."

"Probably."

She opened her eyes, feeling miserable. "So if I don't approve, why can't I stop thinking about them?"

"I'm sorry, Jules. I can't answer that." Kim frowned. Again she hesitated before speaking. "Okay, you want to know what I really think?"

"Of course I want to know. That's the whole purpose of this conversation."

"I think that you should stop this right now. Whatever is going on between the three of you, don't take it any further. You'll ruin the relationships you already have with the two of them. Plus you won't be proud of yourself—not if you're embarrassed by your actions."

Kim was right, of course. Her sister had an uncanny knack of seeing things from a different angle to her. A clearer angle.

Julia dropped her head in her hands. As appealing as the idea might be, sleeping with both men was unacceptable. If Julia had approved, she'd have gone the distance last week. She'd have torn off her clothes, and Hunter's and Jay's, and demanded they all make love right there on Jay's dining room floor.

She hadn't, because that kind of behavior would demand she cross a line she wasn't prepared to cross. Not if she ever wanted to look her parents, or herself, in the eye again.

Julia sat up straight. She knew what she had to do. The

next time she saw Jay and Hunter, her focus would have to be on getting their relationship off the track it had jumped onto last week and back onto neutral ground. If she had any hope of forming a lasting relationship with *one* man, she had to give up the unexpected invitation to sample both of them.

Chapter Three

"Come in, Jules," Hunter invited, looking altogether too good in a pair of jeans that sat low on his hips and framed his powerful thighs beautifully. Not that she was looking there. His T-shirt hugged his shoulders and chest, defining the muscle that bunched in his arms. Not that she was looking there either. For the moment she was through looking at either Hunter or Jay in any meaningful way. Look at the trouble it had gotten her into last week.

"Am I the first one here?" she asked. Silence emanated from the house. Usually a barrage of voices and laughter greeted her arrival. This was the last game of the year. The following Friday's poker was cancelled because of Christmas, and the week after that because it would be New Year's Day.

"Second," Hunter said, not bothering to hide his appraisal of her. He gave her a very slow once-over, his gaze halting at chest height.

Her nipples pebbled.

"Christ," he muttered as he stepped aside to let her in. "I'm getting turned on just looking at you."

Blood warmed her cheeks. Crap, she had to keep this platonic. Had to return their friendship to the point it had been before last Friday night. "Even though I'm wearing glasses?" she tried to tease him.

His brown eyes turned molten. "I hadn't noticed."

Julia shot him an annoyed frown. Damn it, how could she play it cool when he turned her blood to fire with just a glance? "That's because you haven't looked above my neck since I arrived."

He shrugged. "When I'm staring at perfection there's no need to look anywhere else."

Julia shook her head. Oh dear, tonight was going to be even harder than she'd imagined. She wanted to be exasperated by his response, wanted to not blossom beneath his gaze, but his overt reaction delighted her. She walked inside and headed for the lounge room. Her heart drummed wildly and then cartwheeled. Jay sat on the couch.

"Hey," she murmured as heat gathered between her legs.

Shit. Shit, shit, shit. This situation wasn't good for her resolve. Not good at all.

"Jules." His hair was ruffled and he had a sleepy look in his eyes. A sleepy, do-you-want-to-do-naughty-things kind of a look.

Her unvoiced reply was a resounding yes. But then she gave it a second thought, mentally kicked her own butt and changed her answer to no. *Under no circumstances. No, no and no again. Can't and won't cross that line.*

She glanced around the room. "Where are the cards?" The table was bare, with no hint of poker chips either.

"You didn't get the message?" Hunter asked as he followed her into the room.

"What message?"

"The one saying poker was cancelled tonight."

She turned to face him. "Noooo."

Jay chuckled. "That's because we never sent it to you."

Hunter nodded. "Des and the other boys had a late business meeting. They couldn't make it." He paused for a heartbeat. "Lucky for us."

The temperature in the room shot up by at least fifty degrees. This was not good news. Not good news at all. Especially not to a woman who wanted these two men in a way no woman should want two men. "And you decided I didn't need to know this little bit of information?"

"Pretty much." Jay stood and walked over to her.

Every one of her senses clicked to hyper alert. "We can't play if there are only three of us."

"Oh, we can play," Hunter assured her, "just not poker."

Julia's stomach lurched.

"You've been avoiding me this week," Jay said, stepping up close. So close, his breath stirred through her hair.

"Me too. I called a couple of times, but you never answered." Hunter moved to stand behind her. "It's not nice to be ignored."

A thrill of awareness shot through her. "I...I texted you." Her protest came out weak. Once again she was sandwiched between them. She had to clear her throat to speak. "You guys, uh, surprised me at the last game," she confessed, knowing her face was bright pink. "Avoiding you was easier than talking about...what we did."

"What did we do?" Jay asked. His lips whispered over her cheek.

Hot chills ran up her spine. "Th...this."

"Did you like it?" Hunter's mouth was at her ear, his teeth grazing her lobe.

"I—" Lord, how could she tell them she'd loved it when she knew she shouldn't have done it? When she had to avoid doing it again?

Hunter let out a soft breath. The warm air caressed her neck. "You...what?"

A hand crept up her thigh and under the hem of her miniskirt. She had no idea whose hand it was, but its touch generated a massive outbreak of gooseflesh over her butt and legs.

"It was interesting," she conceded at last, doing her best to keep cool. Unfortunately her breath came out in soft pants, and her breasts had tightened against Jay's chest, her nipples proof that the men's actions affected her—yet again.

Jay chuckled. "As interesting as this?" Another hand touched her other leg. This one was bigger than the first one, the touch a little cooler, and its fingers skimmed over her thigh and up to her hip.

Do not cross the line!

God help her, she needed to step away. Needed to extricate herself from the deluge of testosterone that muddled her thoughts and jammed her senses. Needed to look her parents in the eye tomorrow and the next day and the day after that. She put her hands against Jay's chest to push him away but grabbed his shirt and clung for dear life instead.

Heat zinged between her legs, and she would have moaned out loud had her mouth not been taken by Jay's in a heart-pounding kiss.

Hunter pressed his lips to her neck, covering it with sweet, sensual kisses.

How could she resist? How could she push either of them away? For four months she'd been unable to choose one over the other, and here they were taking the choice away from her. Here they were offering her another solution altogether.

She loved two men, and both seemed determined to be with her. How could she not accept them?

Then again, how could she? What would happen to the three of them if she slept with both men at the same time?

But why did kissing them both feel so incredible? So right? Perhaps this was what fate had had in store for her all along. Perhaps she'd never been able to choose one because they were *both* her destiny.

Bullshit. No woman was graced with two men as her destiny. Not in this day and age, in which she and almost every woman she knew, whether career-oriented or not, was raised to want marriage and the customary two-point-six children.

Jay ran his tongue over hers, nipped her lower lip and pulled away.

Aw, fuck. Who cared what every other woman she knew wanted? She yanked at his shirt, pulling him right back to her, and kissed him again.

Hunter growled in her ear. "It's time to up the stakes."

As Jay continued to bamboozle her with exquisite kisses, Hunter moved with a shuffle behind her. The next thing she knew something warm and moist touched the back of her thigh, just below the edge of her skirt.

She trembled. Hunter was on his knees, teasing her legs with his mouth. So focused was she on his seduction and Jay's kiss that she failed to notice the large hand had moved from her hip. It was now on her breast, stroking from the bottom, molding over the curve and caressing her taut nipple.

She groaned against Jay's lips.

Shit. She should not be doing this.

Hunter pushed her skirt up, and his mouth moved over her thigh, heading towards her buttock. When he reached it, he gave a gentle nip.

She jumped. Never mind upping the stakes, Hunter was upping her heart rate to a good sixty *million* beats per minute.

She should leave now, before temptation shoved her right over that line she'd drawn. She should leave with her reputation intact and her heart still in one piece. She pulled away from Jay, preparing to stop all action, but Jay took the opportunity to begin unbuttoning her blouse.

Begin? He was finished before she could draw her next breath. Her shirt hit the floor, followed quickly by her bra, and still Julia hadn't found the voice to protest.

"Christ, Jules," Jay whispered, and trailed his fingertips over her heaving breasts. "You're gorgeous."

Her breath caught. Damn it, she had to get out of there. Before she demanded they strip off their clothes and press their naked flesh against hers. Both of them.

"Boys, please—" Her request went unfinished. Hunter's tongue delved between the cheeks of her butt and she lost the will to protest.

A flood of moisture pooled in her pussy, and she twisted her hips, widening her stance to give Hunter better access. Common sense warned her the action was foolish, but with each shaky breath she took, that common sense faded into oblivion, replaced by a deep-seated need. A hunger that wouldn't quit. A yearning that had begun for Jay a year ago and increased exponentially when she'd met Hunter eight months later. The desire now burned within, a flame that couldn't be extinguished—no matter how much logic dictated she walk away.

She wanted more. More than the touch of the two men. She ached to feel their naked flesh against hers. Both of them were still clothed, while little by little, her garments disappeared.

She tugged on Jay's shirt until he hauled it off.

With a sharp intake of air, Julia registered the sensation of skin against skin, of soft, curly hair against her sensitized nipples.

Hunter's mouth landed on the thin strap of her thong. He traced the material with hot kisses punctuated by moist licks. Down he went, drawing her butt cheeks apart, dipping his tongue where his lips couldn't reach, trailing it over her tender anus and further, until he found her saturated crotch.

She gave a soft sigh as Hunter inhaled, and then his mouth was on her pussy, the lace of her thong the only barrier between his scorching lips and her aching core.

Before she could appreciate the impact of his mouth he'd scooted away, leaving her bereft.

"Hunter..." she complained.

"Jay." Hunter's voice echoed with the same desire that ricocheted through her body. "We need to switch places. Now."

Cool air breezed over bare skin and then Jay stood behind her, his chest pressed against her back as Hunter knelt at her feet. He shoved her skirt above her hips and rolled her thong down her legs. Instead of rolling the thong right back up and walking away like she should have, she kicked the underwear aside.

Thunderstruck by the intensity of her arousal, Julia stood still as the two men put their game plan into action. Jay turned her head to the side and took her mouth in another knee-trembling kiss as his hands found her breasts. Hunter buried his face between her legs, found her clit and sucked it into his mouth, laving it with his tongue.

Unbridled pleasure washed through her. How on earth could she stand like this—between two men—feeling wanton and wicked and desperate for more, when she should be shy, inhibited and awkward, and searching for a means of escape?

She wound one hand through Hunter's hair, letting the silky strands trickle through her fingers. The other hand she clamped over Jay's, holding it over her breast.

Moisture trickled down her inner thigh, and Hunter released her clit to lap at her juices. He followed the rivulets upstream, found its source, and licked her slick folds before dipping his tongue into her pussy.

Julia began to tremble. Perhaps, just for this one night she could give in to her lust and desire and greed and enjoy two of them. *Just this once.* No one beside the three of them need ever know about it.

Jay released her mouth. "Is it good?" he whispered before nipping her earlobe.

Her only reply was a sensual moan.

Jay flicked his thumb over her nipple. "Christ, Jules, I've waited a long time to hold you naked in my arms."

Hunter ran his tongue up to her clit where he swirled it around. "Mmm," he agreed, and she got the distinct impression his hot breath steamed against her pussy. "Me too."

"You...you have?" Astonishment didn't begin to describe her response. "B-both of you?" she managed to gasp out.

"Can't speak for Hunter. But me? Fuck, yeah." Jay nuzzled her chin.

"You taste even better than I thought you would," Hunter told her. "And I've thought about this often." He buried his tongue as deep in her channel as it would go, while Julia's knees trembled beneath her.

Jay dropped his free hand to her ass and brushed his fingers over her crease. She burrowed back into his touch.

"I've fantasized about being with you since that first lunch,"

Jay told her. He slipped one digit between her butt cheeks. "Watching you eat..." He swallowed. "All I could think about was how your mouth would feel on my dick."

Dear God, he'd wanted her for as long as she'd wanted him. Not that knowing would have helped back then. Jay had been involved with someone else. "I-I wondered the...same thing," Julia confessed. Lying to herself, or either of them, seemed impossible under the circumstances. "About...both of you."

Hunter groaned and focused his attention back on her clit.

Jay swore under his breath, and his finger found her anus.

Julia's tremble moved up to full-blown shivering. Jay slipped his finger in her pussy and then bought it back to her ass, now wet and lubricated with her own cream. He massaged the tight ring of muscle until she relaxed enough for him to dip his finger inside.

Any last-minute concerns flew out the window. She crossed over the invisible line as clearly as if she'd taken a physical step. Later she'd cross back. For this moment in time, being here with both men was right. Afterwards she'd face the repercussions of her impulsive actions, but for now she couldn't give a flying hoot. She wanted Jay and Hunter. And God help all three of them, they seemed intent on having her.

"Shit," Hunter gasped. "That is so damn hot." He moved his head away and slipped his own finger inside her pussy. Then he added another—and watched as she twisted first this way then that, desperate to take the men in deeper.

Hunter licked his lips. "Is this what you want, Four Eyes? Both of us in you at the same time?"

Julia tried to answer, but couldn't. Jay had added another finger in her ass and it burned.

"It's okay," Jay whispered. "Take a minute to get used to the stretch." He tweaked her nipple, sending darts of pleasure

171

through her chest.

Julia nodded and breathed around the pain. Slowly it subsided and she relaxed into Jay's touch. Relaxed enough to clench her ass around his two fingers, and her pussy around Hunter's two. "Ah. This gives new meaning to the term holding two pairs." She sighed with pleasure.

Jay chuckled. "That's it, baby," he encouraged her. "Hold us inside you."

Hunter pumped his fingers into her and licked her clit. "Is it what you want, Jules?" he asked again. "Our hands?"

Julia writhed between the two men. "Oh, it's what I want," she answered, out of breath. "This—and so much more."

Hunter stared up at her. "Tell us about the so much more."

Julia would have dropped her head back against Jay's chest but she couldn't stop herself from looking at Hunter. He looked criminally sexy on his knees. His mouth was wet with her juices, and his hand disappeared between her legs. "I want everything, Blondie." She bit at her swollen bottom lip. "I want you to lick me, over and over again, like I've imagined you would—so many times."

Hunter's pupils dilated.

Julia felt another pull of desire. "I want you to lick me while your fingers are inside me. Your fingers and Jay's."

Hunter wasted no time. He lowered his face again and ran his tongue over her clit, up and down, round and round, gentle at first and then with more pressure. At the same time he pumped his fingers into her, waiting for Jay to pull out before he pushed in.

Julia panted with delight. God, this was better than any of the fantasies she'd ever allowed herself. This was real. "That...that's not all." She hesitated for a heartbeat. "W...would you guys be willing to split the pot, so to speak?"

Jay groaned in her ear. "What are you asking, Jules?"

Julia swallowed down the nerves that had formed a lump in her throat. "I...I...want you to fuck me. Both of you. At the same time."

Hunter made a noise that emanated from somewhere deep in his throat. "Sweetheart, if you're the pot, I'll take you any way I can get you."

"Christ," Jay breathed. "Me too." He scissored his fingers in her ass, stretching her, promising her.

Their eagerness to up the ante emboldened her. "Blondie?" she said to Hunter, who'd resumed his exquisite attack on her pussy.

He lifted his head again, focusing his big brown eyes on her face.

"I want you in my ass. All of you. Every inch, buried balls-deep."

He licked his lips and then nodded. "I want me in your ass too, Four Eyes. Every last inch."

A shiver of anticipation sent a fresh set of goosebumps skittering over her skin. She twisted her head around to see Jay. "And you," she said in a scratchy voice, "you I want in my pussy. Deep in my pussy. Way deeper than your fingers could ever reach."

"Whenever you're ready," Jay said hoarsely. "Just say the word."

"I'm ready," Hunter gasped.

Jay chortled. "I was talking to Jules."

"I know," Hunter said and licked her like a man ravenous for a good meal.

"I'm ready," Julia agreed. Either that—or she was going to

come, and if she exploded now, it would be a long time before she could summon up the energy to start again. Jay and Hunter had her so hot, her orgasm was sure to hit with monumental force.

"Oh, Jesus." Jay's voice was rough enough to be nonexistent. "This is gonna happen. We're really gonna do it."

Instead of disagreeing, Julia asked, "Do you have any condoms?"

Hunter gave her a final kiss on her clit and drew away. "A box full," he said as he stood. "In my bedroom."

Before she could head in that direction, Hunter kissed her. A full, open-mouthed kiss that made her dizzy. He tasted of man and of Hunter and of sex—her sex, and she drank from him thirstily. Then she turned to Jay and kissed him in the same fashion. Her head swam, her body burned and desire tugged her between her legs, making her moan into Jay's mouth.

"Bedroom. Now!" Hunter demanded, ending the kiss.

She followed Hunter through the house, watching as he stripped his clothes off along the way. His shirt came first, followed by his jeans and boxers, which he kicked off as he reached his bedroom door. Julia stopped to take in the firmness of his extraordinary butt, and noticed a faded, thin scar that ran along one cheek.

Jay walked into her from behind, distracting her.

The feel of hot flesh against her bare bottom told her he'd pulled off his own pants on the way. His rigid cock poked her spine, leaving tiny drops of moisture on her back.

"Boys," she said in a throaty voice. "I need you to fuck me. Now."

Jay lifted her up from behind and carried her to Hunter's

bed. He laid her down and knelt on the floor in front of her.

"My turn," he said, and dipped his head to lick her pussy.

"Hunter!" Julia groaned in desperation as sensation hit her. "Damn it, get that condom on, or it'll be over before you're even inside me." Shoot, she was close. So bloody close she wasn't sure she could hold on.

Hunter turned to her. His proud erection stood thick between his legs. It was slightly curved and sheathed with a condom. In his hand he held a tube of lubricant and a second condom.

On second thought, she *would* hold on. She'd do anything to get that cock inside her.

"It's on, Four Eyes," he assured her and sat on the bed. "You chose well. I'm an ass man," he said, and proceeded to coat his condom with lube. "Nothing I'd like more than to explore your hot back end with my dick."

Julia clenched her ass, wanting nothing more than for Hunter to fuck her from behind.

Jay released her clit from his heavenly mouth. "And I am more than happy to take possession of your pussy, Jules. Permanently." His eyes shone with heated promise.

Okay, there was something she wanted more than Hunter fucking her from behind: Hunter fucking her from behind while Jay fucked her from the front.

Sweet heaven. If Julia got much wetter she'd slide right off the bed.

Hunter tossed the second condom to Jay and lay down on his back. He idly pumped his dick, spreading the lube all over it.

Julia's mouth watered.

"Come here, Four Eyes," he said in a wicked voice. "Come

straddle my chest and show me that tempting ass."

Julia tugged the skirt over her hips and threw it to the floor, then did what Hunter requested. She straddled his chest—his muscled, powerful chest—and leaned forward, facing Jay, so her ass was tilted towards Hunter's face.

"Fuck, yeah," Hunter muttered. He bit her buttock as something cold and wet touched her anus.

The breath left her lungs in a hiss.

Jay put his right knee on the bed, next to Hunter's left leg, offering Julia an enticing view of his cock. Pausing only to remove her glasses and set them on the bedside table, she leaned forward and licked the head of Jay's dick, tasting the salty beads of precome. The tip of Hunter's lubed penis rubbed against her chin.

All three of them moaned.

Julia's head swam. It was happening. She was here, with both of them. She was about to make love to Jay and Hunter. Never would she have believed ending up in bed with the *two* men she loved could become a reality.

Hunter took the opportunity to massage lube around her ass, probing her hole to lubricate that too. As his fingers pushed inside her, she took Jay's cock deeper into her mouth, sucking and licking him, feasting. She loved his taste, loved the smooth way his velvety skin rubbed against her tongue.

As she lowered her head to lick a testicle, she used one hand to support herself and the other to stroke Hunter's dick. She sighed in satisfaction. Perfect. Absolute perfection. Both of them.

She looked up at Jay's face and found his gaze fixed on her mouth. His lips had formed an O shape and his pupils were dilated.

"Fuck, Jules," Hunter rasped. "Enough teasing. I want you on my cock. Now."

Hands held her around her waist, pulling her into a sitting position. She let go of Jay's penis with a wet slurp and watched with hunger as he donned a condom. His erection was long and thick, like the rest of him, and the thought of it in her pussy made her ache with need.

Hunter's hands left her waist and landed on her butt. "Scooch forward," he told her, and she did, positioning herself above his groin.

"Use your hands, Jules." Hunter's voice was a low growl. "Help guide me inside."

Julia gripped his cock and rubbed the tip against her soaking pussy. She couldn't restrain the soft groan that escaped as his dick massaged her sensitive labia. God, she could come just like this, just by teasing herself.

Or she could come with two stiff penises inside her.

No contest.

Semidazed by her own actions, she rocked forward, bringing her ass in line with Hunter's cock. He assisted her by drawing her cheeks apart. And then ever so slowly, holding Hunter's cock firm, and under Jay's heated gaze, she lowered herself down. Even with the lube and the men's careful preparation, his shaft was larger than their fingers, and she had to bite back a shriek as he penetrated her. It burned. She closed her eyes, warding off the pain.

"You are so fucking sexy," Jay said. "Christ, watching you take Hunter in your ass like that..." His voice wavered. "I could come just looking at the two of you."

She opened her eyes and found herself staring at Jay's hand, which was folded around the base of his cock.

"Have to squeeze tight," he told her, "so I don't climax here and now."

A wave of wild lust gripped Julia. Heaven help her, she wanted Jay. Now. She twisted her hips, impaling herself on Hunter, and bit back a cry of pain and of rapture.

"That's it, Jules," Hunter soothed her from behind. "I'm in all the way. And God, you feel like heaven." He moved, just a little, and the pain subsided somewhat, followed immediately by a flash of pleasure. "Heaven," he said again and caressed her buttocks.

Goosebumps covered her arms and breasts. Cautiously she lifted up and sat back down, experimenting. *Good. Jesus, it felt good.* Sore, but good. She did it again and again.

"Jules." Hunter breathed her name. "Woman, you are every one of my fantasies come to life."

She wanted to answer, wanted to tell him he was all that to her and more, but the only sound that came out of her mouth was a wanton sigh.

Jay shook his head in awe. "You're every man's fantasy, baby," he said. "How the hell did Hunter and I get so lucky?"

She was the lucky one. Not them.

Hands moved from her ass to her waist and then higher to her ribs. They pulled her back until she lay on Hunter. Julia dropped her hands to the bed to give herself support—and to lift her upper body slightly so she could watch as Jay placed a foot beside her on the mattress and leaned forward.

Hunter surged into her from below then withdrew. The breath left her body. She'd never felt anything like it before, never done it in this position. It was freaking amazing, and only improved when Jay directed his dick to her pussy. As he made contact, she froze, enjoying the friction. Even Hunter seemed to sense the momentousness of the occasion, and he stilled as well.

"Do it," Julia urged Jay, opening her legs to him while balancing on Hunter. "Fuck me."

And he did. He edged into her, filling her bit by bit until he too was embedded deep inside her.

Julia breathed in and out, in and out. Full. She was so full. Stuffed to overflowing. She had two erect penises inside her. And by God, Hunter was right. It felt like heaven. Full—and divine.

She twisted her hips. She couldn't move much in this position, but she must have been able to move enough, because the motion yielded gasps from both men. She grinned and did it again. This time the gasp came from her too. Each twist sent her clit scraping against Jay's hair and pubic bone, offering Julia an entire range of stimulation. Her ass, her pussy and her clit were all being subjected to extreme, delectable sensations. Pain and pleasure combined, the contrast of the sensations making the pain more real and the pleasure more intense. Much, much more intense.

Hunter thrust into her at the exact moment Jay pulled out, and when Hunter pulled back, Jay pushed in again. Over and over they moved, each fucking her to distraction, filling her with bliss.

This, here, was the single most profound sexual experience of her life, made all the more incredible because Julia loved Hunter and Jay. If she'd felt anything less for either of them, she'd never have crossed that line, never have trusted them to do what she allowed them to do now. She'd given herself to both of them, body and soul. In a million years she could not picture herself doing this with any other men.

But Jay and Hunter... *Mmm hmm.* If real life never intruded again, she could imagine herself doing this at least once every day—maybe even more.

Hunter's hand strayed to her breast, brushing her nipple. Jay watched as she pushed her chest into Hunter's palm, demanding a harder caress. Hunter pinched her nipple, and her body tightened in response, her reaction ricocheting all the way through to her groin. She clenched her pussy muscles around Jay, who cried out and thrust deep into her without waiting for Hunter to pull out.

She gasped.

"Oh, Christ," Hunter breathed. "Holy shit. Don't move."

Jay froze, all his muscles pulled taut in an effort not to stir. Almost idly, Julia noticed the six-pack lining his stomach and the perspiration beading on his brow. From this close, even without her glasses, she could see the willpower it took for Jay to keep still. His jaw was set and he stared blindly past her.

Or maybe he stared at Hunter, she wasn't sure.

Hunter panted beneath her. "So close," he whispered. "So, so close. One move from either of you, and I am gonna blow my load."

Julia's pussy throbbed. "You mean one move like this, Blondie?" She squeezed her ass cheeks together.

Hunter jerked into her in reaction.

"Fuck," he swore, and Julia felt him stiffen beneath her, his entire body growing tense.

"Or one like this," Jay asked with a quick grin and pulled out then thrust back into her. Then his face twisted, as though the joke was on him and he thrust again and then again. "Jesus, Jules. Can't stop. You feel too...fucking...good." He pumped into her wildly. "Can't...stop. Don't want...to."

"Jay, you bastard," Hunter swore, and then he too was driving into her as hard as he could in his position.

Julia's breath hitched and caught. Sweet Lord, she was being pulled in all directions, unadulterated pleasure flowing through her pussy, her clit and her ass. Showering her with delight and with pain.

"Can't stop it," Hunter yelled as he clamped his hands around her waist and thrust into her one last time. She felt him pulse in her ass, over and over, releasing inside her. "Oh, God, Jules," he moaned. *"Juliaaaaa."*

Sensation swamped her, knocking her for a loop. She lost control, and came hard, months' worth of pent-up desire escaping as her pussy spasmed in relief.

Jay stared first at her and then at Hunter, and then he too lost control and jerked into Julia. He threw his head back and howled when he came, his hips shaking as he emptied himself in her pussy.

Minutes passed before any of them could move. Finally, Jay pulled out of her, tossed the condom in the bin and collapsed on the bed. "Holy shit." He whistled. "Why'd we never do that before?"

Hunter rolled over with Julia in his arms, carefully withdrawing from her at the same time. He too trashed his condom, then curled up on his side behind her, pressing in close, so they both faced Jay. "Beats me. But I'm almost ready to do it again."

Julia sighed. Her limbs were heavy, her heart still racing. "You do this together often, boys?"

Jay snickered. "You mean sleep with you? Nope, baby. Like we said, we're wondering why we'd never done it before."

"Smartass." She smiled lazily. "I mean threesomes. You do it a lot?"

"It's a first for me," Hunter said as he drew his hand over her waist.

"Me too." Jay nodded.

Julia closed her eyes. "I liked it." She shouldn't have, but she had. Altogether too much.

"So did I," Hunter said.

"I think I just found a new favorite poker hand," Jay laughed. "Three of a kind."

Julia blanched. Three of a kind worked for her too. Altogether too well. So how the hell did she step back over that invisible line now? Knowing her luck, she'd trip and fall the minute she tried.

Chapter Four

"C'mon, darl', have another helping."

Julia eyed the dish her aunt offered her and finally gave in. So what if she was stuffed? Nobody made shrimp on the barbie like her dad and her Uncle Joe, and anyway it was Christmas. She was supposed to eat until her belly ached. Besides, if her mouth was full she wouldn't be expected to talk. Good thing too, because if one more relative asked her when it was *her turn*, she would throw up. Right in the middle of the traditional family Chrissie lunch.

It was her cousin Alec's fault. If he hadn't chosen today to announce his engagement, she wouldn't be the subject of everyone's curiosity. So what if she was a year older than Alec and thus expected to marry before him? Twenty-eight was hardly ancient. She wasn't over-the-hill yet. She still had plenty of time to find the right man and settle down.

Sure her family liked to pry, but they only asked about her nonexistent nuptials because they loved her and wanted her to be happy. In the Savage family's opinion, happiness meant love and marriage. It meant children and tradition. It didn't mean one woman sleeping with two men at the same time.

She bit off a piece of shrimp and chewed it viciously.

"So, Julia," her great-aunt Edith said, "when are you going to give the family some good news? Isn't it time you settled down and got married too?"

Julia secretly blessed the shrimp, and pointed to her mouth, making it obvious she couldn't answer. She kicked her sister under the table.

Kim snorted softly.

"Get them to change the freaking subject," Julia ground out around her food.

"Don't look at me to save you," Kim whispered. Her lips did not move. "You chose two instead of one. Even I can't help you through this dilemma."

Julia swallowed and then shoved the remaining shrimp in her mouth, chewing it stiffly. She stood and proceeded to clear the table of empty dishes. Stretching over her sister, she murmured, "Sisters are supposed to stand up for one another— regardless of the circumstances."

Kim pushed back her chair and helped Julia take the plates to the kitchen. "Jules," she said, once both of them had made sure no one else was in the room, "I love you dearly, but even I'm not brave enough to stand up to Aunt Edith."

"Hah!" *Coward.* "Just for that I'm going back in there and asking when you plan on having your next baby."

Kim's jaw dropped. "You wouldn't."

Julia shrugged and smiled innocently. "Try me."

Kim smiled right back, her evil big-sister smile. "Open your mouth and I'm taking my earrings back. And the jeans you borrowed from me last month."

Oh no. No way was she returning those jeans. "Fine," she conceded, "but just wait 'til you ask me to babysit again."

"Cow," Kim shot at her, and the two of them began to giggle.

At least Kim was still talking to her. She'd been terrified her sister would crap on her for going ahead and sleeping with Jay and Hunter against her better advice.

Embarrassed to tell anyone she was sleeping with two men, Julia would have kept it a secret, but Kim had taken one look at her face and guessed at the truth. Within ten minutes of seeing her today, Julia had explained the situation to her. What had started as a just-this-once deviation from her regular relationship with Jay and Hunter had somehow turned into a once-every-night-this-week-and-often-much-more-than-that plus once-every-morning-after-as-well deviation.

So much for the promise she'd made to herself to cross back over that invisible line after their first time. She'd failed miserably at keeping it.

She, Jay and Hunter had spent every free minute together since their cancelled poker evening last Friday, and the sex was only getting better. They'd made love in all three of their homes, but in the end kept returning to Hunter's because his bed was the biggest, leaving lots of room for their more...active sessions.

The more they made love, the more natural the act itself became. But that, it seemed to Julia, was the only natural part of their new and much more complicated relationship.

Yes, the sex was over-the-top incredible. Yes, she was crazy about both men, and yes, she turned to mush every time she saw either of them. But no, their relationship didn't sit comfortably with her.

A part of her awaited the inevitable repercussions of her lust. She half expected a lightning bolt to blast through the sky and strike her for her sins. Well, not really, but she still hadn't reconciled the Julia who was expected to get married and have children someday with the Julia who wanted sex with Hunter and Jay all the time.

"So," Kim said softly when their laughter faded, "I know

you're in no hurry to introduce your men to Mom and Dad. But what about me? Do I get to meet them?"

Julia stared at her, bewildered. Kim had met all of her boyfriends up until now. Yet the idea of introducing not one, but two men to her sister freaked Julia out.

That wasn't the only thing bothering her. If Kim wanted to meet the guys, she must be assuming their threesome would continue for an indeterminate length of time. Surely such an unconventional relationship was doomed to die a hasty death? Without the support of their loved ones, how could it survive? She, Jay and Hunter would have to fight long and hard to get their families on their side, and Julia didn't know if either man was willing to commit to such a battle.

"I...I'm not sure I'm ready for that," she finally said.

"I can understand your hesitancy," Kim sympathized. "If I'm struggling with the idea of you having two guys in your bed, you must be going insane trying to come to terms with it."

"You have no idea," Julia said, grateful for Kim's insight.

Her sister tapped her lip thoughtfully. "Okay, I don't want to rush you, so I have another idea. New Year's Eve is a week away, right?"

Julia nodded, and wondered if she, Hunter and Jay would celebrate together.

"If you're still..." Kim wavered, looking uncertain. "Uh, seeing them then, and if you're more secure in your...relationship, would you consider introducing me on the first of January? We could look at it as a new start to a new year."

A pang whacked Julia in the stomach. What if she wasn't still seeing them? The thought filled her with dread and gloom. But then, considering all the odds they faced, continuing their alternative arrangement into the New Year terrified her. All she

186

knew for sure was that she couldn't wait to get back to Hunter's place after lunch. Couldn't wait to see them both again. But that was as far into the future as she'd considered.

"It's not a bad plan," Julia told Kim. "But let's just play this whole introduction stuff by ear. We can speak on the first and decide then what to do depending on the circumstances. Okay?"

Kim regarded her thoughtfully. "Okay, little sis. I just hope the circumstances turn out the way you want them to. The way that'll make you happiest."

And therein lay Julia's biggest problem. She had no idea how said circumstances would turn out.

Chapter Five

Julia relaxed in the bath, swirls of steam spiraling above her. In the bedroom next door Jay lay fast asleep, while Hunter took a shower in the glassed stall beside the bath.

Julia watched as Hunter soaped himself and shampooed his hair, wishing she could focus on the sleek movement of his muscles as he washed. But without her glasses she couldn't see her own toes clearly beneath the water. Still the scent of his lemony shampoo wound its way through her nose, making her hungry for a taste of him.

Ah, crap. Truth was, she was never not hungry for him or Jay.

What now? Where did they go from here? Her conversation with Kim at lunch had her anxious. No matter how uncertain she was about the future of this threesome, one thing she had no doubts about were her feelings for the men. She was seriously in love with both of them. Enough in love that the thought of ever finding anyone else was ridiculous. Julia knew that after Jay and Hunter no other man could ever come close. No one else could compete. She'd suspected it months before anything had happened between them. Their last week together had cemented her convictions.

But her convictions only complicated issues. What would Hunter and Jay say if they knew her feelings towards them went way beyond sexual desire? Sure, they knew she found them both irresistible, but apart from physical satisfaction, none of them had discussed the emotional side of things. They were too busy having sex.

"You know what, Four Eyes?" Hunter said as he stepped out of the shower.

I know I love you. "Tell me."

Hunter toweled himself dry. "You are some kind of wonderful."

She grinned at him.

"Smart, sassy, sexy and beautiful. And a tigress in bed."

She couldn't be sure, but she thought he smiled.

"You're pretty good in bed yourself, Blondie."

He wrapped the towel around his waist and came to sit on the side of the bath. "Is this all okay for you?" The concern in his voice was unmistakable. "You know, being with both of us?"

Had he read her mind? "Okay?" She laughed lightly. "It's freaking amazing."

He was close enough for her to notice his frown at her answer. "You're lying," he said in a soft voice. "You've been too quiet this evening. Is something bothering you?"

Damn eyes of his. They saw way too much. She sighed. "I am lying."

"What's the problem?"

Julia bit her lip, but said nothing.

"Are we too much for you? Both...both of us together? Jay and I were worried about that."

"God, no!" Julia knew her answer left no room for doubt. "I love making love to both of you. Love, love, love it." Even talking about it got her hot, and she squirmed in the water, her body tightening in awareness.

Hunter's gaze caught on her breasts and stayed there for a couple of seconds. When he spoke again, his voice was gruff. He had to stop and clear his throat. "So what's the matter?"

Oh Lord, how did she explain this?

"Jules, I've licked your ass. I've fucked you in every way known to mankind. And I'll be damned if I don't want to do it over and over again." He took a shaky breath. "We're past the point of pretending to be shy around each other. If you're worried about something, tell me. Let me help." Hunter trailed a hand in the water.

She gave him a half smile. "Well, when you put it like that..." She gnawed on her bottom lip. "Are you comfortable with the way things have turned out between the three of us?"

He thought about her question. Emotion flashed in his eyes, but she couldn't identify it. "Surprised would be a more accurate description."

She snorted. "Oh, I can relate to that."

"I never thought I'd enjoy sharing you with another man, but with Jay—" He hesitated, as though he were measuring each word. "I like it. A lot." He swept his hand along her ribs and up over her breast. Her nipple beaded in response.

"I like it a lot too." Julia licked her lips. "More than I ever imagined I would."

"I'd always wanted you to myself," Hunter told her. "Up until that first night we kissed, I hadn't..." Again he paused. "I hadn't thought this could be an option."

Julia blushed. "I fantasized about both of you—all the time, but in my wildest dreams I never saw the *three* of us together."

Hunter's eyes darkened, hunger shadowing his expression.

"The reality is pretty different from the fantasies," Julia

mused.

"Do you regret the reality?" he asked.

"No. I wasn't kidding earlier. I love making love to both of you."

"So why do you look so worried?"

Because I love our threesome but fear nothing can become of it. Because I always imagined myself with either you or Jay, and now that I've had you both I have no idea how to adapt to the circumstances. Because the thought of my family finding out about you two scares the crap out of me. "My, er, sister wants to meet you."

Hunter looked surprised. "She knows about us?"

Julia nodded. "As soon as she saw my face today she knew something was up. She demanded I tell her what."

Hunter nodded and sat up straight. "Family is sharp that way. My mother asked too."

It was Julia's turn to register surprise. "About me and Jay?"

"Not quite." Hunter looked uneasy. "She wanted to know if I'd *met someone.*" He used his fingers to quote his mother's words.

She could relate to his discomfort. She was troubled by the idea of telling her parents about Jay and Hunter. He must feel the same way. "And what did you say?"

He regarded her for a long time before answering. "I told her I had."

Her heart lurched. Hunter had thought their relationship important enough to tell his mother.

"But I didn't say anything else. I wasn't ready to speak about it."

Julia gave a little snort. "Yeah. Not such an easy topic to

191

broach with family, is it?"

"Nope. It's not every day you share the news that you and a mate are sleeping with the same woman—together."

"Try telling your family two men are sharing you."

He raised an eyebrow and smiled.

She laughed. "Was your mother okay with your not giving her details?"

He nodded. "She's pretty cool that way."

"Sounds like the two of you are close," Julia mused.

Hunter shrugged. "We are now."

"You weren't always?"

He shifted in discomfort. "We had our issues. It took a while, but we've sorted them out."

Hunter had told her a few days ago that his parents had divorced when he was a teenager. His father had not been very involved in his life since then, and apparently Hunter preferred it that way.

"Are you going to tell her about us?" she asked.

"Maybe." He turned the question back on her. "Are you going to introduce us to Kim?"

Julia frowned. "I...I don't know. It's all too...soon to tell. We decided to talk about it again on New Year's Day, and see how I felt then."

Hunter was quiet for a long while. "You know, I'd be happy to meet her," he said at last. "If you're ready to introduce us."

Warmth suffused her. "And if I'm not ready?"

"I'm happy to wait."

The warmth turned to heat. Damn, she loved him. Full-on, head-over-heels loved him. "You know what, Blondie?"

"Nope. Tell me," Hunter invited.

"You're some kind of wonderful."

His eyes glinted. "I know, I know. Smart, sassy, sexy and beautiful. And a tigress in bed."

She chuckled at the thought. Hunter was as male as men came. Hot, hard, dominant, alpha and masculine through and through. And the man in him called out to the woman in her. The muscles in her pussy clenched as desire tugged at them.

"You up to showing me your tigress skills now?" she invited.

"I'm up for it anytime," Hunter answered, his voice sinful as sex.

The air around them changed. Awareness sparked between them.

The bathroom door opened and Jay walked in.

Julia's heart skipped a beat. His timing was impeccable. How'd he known to join them just as things heated up?

"Hey, baby," Jay said. "You're looking good in there. Good and naked."

She undulated her hips as her desire grew. "Hey, sleepyhead," she answered. "We've been talking about you."

Jay was as naked as she was—with the exception of the Santa hat on his head. "Saying good things, I hope?"

"Very good." Lust raced through her veins. "Hunter just told me he likes sharing me with you."

Jay growled a deep, sensual growl.

"I think my exact words were, 'I like it. *A lot.*'" Hunter dipped his hand back in the bath and ran his finger along the curve of her breast, making her shiver. Warm water rippled around her skin.

"I love sharing you too, baby. I love fucking you, knowing Hunter's doing the same. Feeling his cock in there, near mine, is a huge turn-on. Massive." He walked over to the bath. His erection was growing by the second. Jay stood close enough to Hunter that his hip brushed the blond man's arm.

Hunter jerked away as if he'd been burned.

"Are you okay?" Julia asked.

Hunter rubbed his biceps. "Uh, yeah. Fine."

"You sure?" He didn't look fine.

"Jay just gave me a shock. There must be static in the air or something." Cautiously he returned his arm to rest against Jay's hip. "That's better."

"It's all the electricity snapping between us and Jules," Jay joked. His gaze was trained on her breast and Hunter's hand.

Damn, she wanted to lick Jay's erection all over. She wanted to feel both of them inside her, both of them fucking her. "Whatever it is snapping between us, I like it. I love being shared between you."

Julia looked at the point where the men's bodies touched. Her men's bodies. Touching. Just like that she lost her breath.

There it was again, the hunger to taste them, consume them. It seemed her desire for Jay and Hunter knew no boundaries. It just multiplied and expanded on a daily basis.

Hunter drew his hand over her belly, stopping above the curls on her pussy. Jay muttered something unintelligible.

When she could inhale again, she looked at them through a lusty haze. "Boys, are you just going to hang around there and watch me bathe?"

Hunter dragged his fingers through the curls. "You have any better ideas?" His muscles bunched in his arms as he moved, and Jay drew in a sharp breath.

"I sure do. See, I'm looking to create a lot more sparks between us." Desire seeped through her, trickling into every cell in her body. "How about you jump in the shower, Jay, and get all nice and clean? When you're done, come on out of the bathroom and watch me..." She paused, looked at Hunter and licked her lips. "Watch me suck Blondie's cock into my mouth."

Hunter's hand stilled. His eyes turned black as night.

She looked in Jay's direction. The desire in his expression made her swallow before she could talk again. "Y-you never know what else may develop from there."

Jay yanked off his hat and threw it on the bathroom counter. "Get out of the bath and get dried, Jules." Lust masked whatever humor she'd expected to hear in Jay's voice. "I'll be done here in two minutes. I expect to see you on your knees on the carpet when I walk into the bedroom."

She made sure that was exactly how Jay found her. On her knees, on the carpet, with her lips wrapped around Hunter's shaft.

God, he tasted good. Clean and musky, with an occasional salty drop for flavor.

Hunter lay on the bed with his legs hanging over the side. His upper body rested on his arms so he could watch Julia at work. The air was filled with his soft, encouraging murmurs.

Julia's one hand held the base of his penis, the other caressed his balls. His cock was slightly thicker than Jay's, but just as delectable.

Julia felt someone's gaze on her back and turned to find Jay standing butt-naked by the bathroom door.

"Fuck," he swore hoarsely and strode over to the bed where he dropped to his knees beside Julia.

She swirled her tongue around the tip of Hunter's dick,

watching Jay's face the entire time.

"Jesus, Jules," Jay gasped. "If I thought I fancied you before, I reckon I'm falling in love with you now." He did not take his gaze off her mouth.

Her heart lurched beneath her breast, but she forced herself not to get too excited by his words, no matter how much she loved him. After all, they were being said in the heat of passion. Nevertheless, still holding Hunter's cock in her hand, she lifted her face to Jay's, inviting him to kiss her.

He did so, hungrily, and when he pulled away and motioned for her to return to Hunter, her lips were swollen and puffy.

Hunter let out a loud groan. "I reckon I'm falling pretty damn hard myself."

He dropped backwards onto the bed as Julia sucked his cock into her mouth again, tickled pink by his confession. She loved Hunter too. She had for the last four months. Once again she warned herself not to get her hopes up. There was very little a man wouldn't say when a woman knelt at his feet.

Hunter flung an arm over his eyes and thrust his hips upwards, filling her mouth. She had to relax every muscle in her throat to fit his dick in.

Jay breathed heavily beside her. "Watching you blow Hunter is giving me a hard-on from hell."

Julia smiled around Hunter's shaft and stilled his movements with her hand. She drew away from him then dipped her head back to lick off the precome that leaked from his cock head. Without swallowing, she turned back to Jay and offered him her mouth. She was mildly surprised by the greed with which Jay kissed her, licking the offering from her tongue. Mildly surprised and majorly aroused.

She squeezed another drop from Hunter and repeated the

process. This time when Jay's lips met hers, he groaned low in his throat.

Keeping her gaze on Jay's face, she held Hunter's dick in her hand and licked it from the base up to the tip and then back down again. Twice she did it, and then a third time, conscious of Jay staring, his eyes glazed with hunger.

Perhaps it took her a few seconds to see the truth because her glasses were off. But once she noticed it, she couldn't deny the fact. It wasn't just her mouth Jay ogled. It was Hunter's penis as well. Hunter's delectable penis.

She licked the head of his dick and then paused to watch Jay.

He licked his lips.

She did it again.

He licked his lips again.

Her pussy tightened.

Jay wanted Hunter's dick.

Ever so slowly she raised her head. While still holding Hunter's shaft, she tilted it, offering it to Jay.

Jay didn't move an inch. Indecision flashed across his face, made obvious by his frown.

Julia pursed her lips and sucked Hunter into her mouth, sliding her lips up and down, making him mumble on the bed. She watched Jay while she feasted.

He watched Hunter's dick.

When he bit his lower lip and his tongue flashed over it, soothing the reddened spot, Julia pulled away, and once again offered him Hunter's penis.

This time he faltered for a second. Then he leaned over and swiped his tongue over the tip of the proffered cock.

Blood raced to Julia's head, making her dizzy. In her entire life she had never seen anything as mesmerizing.

Jay did it again and then again.

Hunter writhed and his hips surged up, as though asking for more.

Jay obliged. Tentatively he opened his mouth and lowered his lips over Hunter's shaft. They touched Julia's fingers, and she released her grasp on Hunter, giving Jay free rein.

Hunter let out a long breath. His arm still covered his eyes, but his lower body was moving now, thrusting up into Jay's mouth.

God, Julia thought, stunned. She was watching Jay go down on Hunter. A man on a man. The one man she loved doing the other man she loved. It was shocking. Scandalous. It was outrageous. And fascinating. And hot. Oh, dear Lord, the very sight turned her on almost more than sleeping with both of them did.

Julia pushed her hand against her pussy, hoping to ease the sudden ache between her legs. Desire burned within, growing hotter as Jay devoured Hunter. Jay's face was a study in concentration. His eyes were closed, as though he relished the experience. With each bob of his head, Jay's confidence seemed to grow, his movements became faster, his expression more intent.

She closed her other hand around Jay's penis, stunned to find it harder than ever, with a vein pulsing tangibly through it.

"Jules," Hunter cried. "Fuck, Jules!" he flung his head from side to side, his eyes still closed. "That feels unbelievable."

Jay froze. His eyes popped open.

"*No.*" Hunter panted. "Christ, don't stop."

Jay stared at her aghast.

Hunter's hips surged up, and Jay was wrenched back into action. He returned his attention to Hunter, his actions so sensual Julia found herself wishing she were on the receiving end of his mouth's exploits.

"That's it," Hunter moaned. "Oh, God. I'm gonna...come. Don't stop. Oh...God."

Hunter began to spasm, his hips jerking against Jay's mouth.

Watching Hunter's orgasm was so exhilarating, so stimulating, she could come herself. All it would take was one swipe of a finger across her clit. She yanked her hand away from her pussy. No way would she come this way. Not when the men of her fantasies could offer so much more.

Jay closed his eyes, extreme satisfaction glowing in his face as he accepted everything Hunter pumped into his mouth.

Several seconds passed before Hunter relaxed and collapsed on the bed. It was then that Jay swallowed, twice, without releasing Hunter's cock.

"Oh, fuck," Hunter gasped. "Jules, Jesus," he said in a scratchy voice. "That was the best damn blowjob I've ever had."

Again Jay looked at her, startled.

Julia inhaled and then climbed on the bed to kneel beside Hunter. She kissed his cheek. "Not Jules, Blondie. Jay."

His eyes flew open. He stared at her in disbelief before pushing up to observe his waist. The evidence he faced was indisputable. At Hunter's sudden movement, his cock slid out of Jay's mouth.

Jay wiped his lips, looked up at Hunter and grinned. "Hey, mate," he said. "You don't taste half bad."

Chapter Six

"The hell I'll calm down," Hunter snarled as he paced the length of the living room. "Goddammit, he gave me a fucking blowjob."

He'd paused long enough to pull on his jeans before storming out of the bedroom, furious. Jay had tried to go after him, but woman's intuition told Julia Hunter wouldn't want to see his friend. So she'd convinced Jay to stay put, and she'd gone instead, pulling Jay's T-shirt on in the process. It hung down to her knees.

"The best blowjob you've ever had," Julia reminded him now, desperate to pacify him. She'd never seen Hunter lose his cool like this. Ever. If either of the men was prone to blowing his top in a stressful situation it was Jay. Yet here Hunter was, way beyond the point of reason.

"Fuck, Jules. You know I thought it was you. Not...not him!"

"But it was him, Hunter. It was Jay. And it was beautiful. The sexiest thing I've ever seen."

Hunter blanched. "It is not *sexy* when one man puts another man's dick in his mouth. It's abnormal. It...it's twisted."

"And two men sleeping with one woman at the same time isn't?" she asked. "You think you can classify a threesome as normal behavior? Hell, I let you *and* Jay fuck me. It's not the kind of thing I'd refer to as regular kind of sex. But you don't seem to see *that* as twisted or wrong. You said, not half an hour ago, that you liked it. A lot."

"We make love to *you*, not to each other. It's a man with a woman, or two men with a woman. Not a man with a man."

"There is nothing wrong with two men together," Julia insisted. She believed that one hundred percent. Especially now, after seeing Jay and Hunter together. Far from being wrong, it seemed both alluring and right.

"There is when one of those men is me." He stabbed his chest with his finger for emphasis. "I like women, Jules, not men. Not Jay."

"You like him well enough when his naked penis is in me, right beside yours."

"His...his dick is separated from mine by you."

"Yet how often is Jay the one who makes you come?" she pointed out calmly, although she felt anything but. "Soon as he increases the pace of our lovemaking, you lose control."

Hunter collapsed into a dining room chair and *thunked* the table hard with his fist. "Fuck it. This is so not what I imagined. I can't do this."

Julia's stomach dropped. The best sexual experience of her life was turning into an unmitigated disaster. Hunter was on the verge of throwing it all away because of Jay's actions.

Her mind raced. A million thoughts bombarded her at once. Desperation merged with misery, resulting in unexpected revelations. Julia was about to lose everything—Hunter, Jay and the incredible intimacy the three of them had created together. The certainty and the horror combined to give her a startling moment of clarity. Suddenly she knew what she wanted. *And it wasn't what she—or her family—expected.*

Julia wanted Jay and Hunter. Both of them. For as long as they'd have her. Her goals and her focus had changed. She'd changed. Jay and Hunter had changed her. Her focus was no longer on choosing one man, it was now about keeping two of them. Together, Jay and Hunter had become the present and the future she desired. The present and future she'd have to fight for—and damn it, she was willing to fight.

It was up to her to sort out this business. To get Hunter to accept that what Jay had done wasn't as perverse as he seemed to think it was.

"It's not a bad thing, Blondie." Julia lowered her voice. "When you come, I come too."

He glowered at her.

"Hunter—" Julia walked over to him, "—whatever is happening between the three of us, it's wonderful. The best experience of my life. The best sex too. Having you and Jay inside me... God, I love it. I never want it to end. I want the three of us to go on forever."

Hunter shook his head. "The three of us are over, Jules." He grimaced. "I don't think I'll ever be able to get a hard-on again if Jay is anywhere near me. If you and I sleep together, it'll be just the two of us. Full stop."

Julia might as well have collided with a brick wall. The impact of his words almost broke her. Hunter was dead serious, as was evident from the set of his shoulders and the determination in his face.

Damn it, she wouldn't let Hunter destroy this magic between them. Not over a blowjob. "Jay liked having you in his mouth," she said, not to goad him, but to make a point. "He liked it a lot. His dick was hard as steel while he blew you." She flexed her fingers, recalling the texture of Jay's shaft, the satiny skin covering the iron-like rod beneath.

"I'll tell you something else," Julia rushed on. "He didn't mean for it to happen. He came to be with me, not to touch you. But one thing led to another and I encouraged him, and the next thing—"

"You encouraged him?" Hunter cut her off, outraged.

She nodded. "You bet I did. He couldn't get enough of your taste when he kissed me, I figured he'd prefer to sample your merchandise firsthand." She shrugged. "I was right. And you preferred it too."

"Bullshit," Hunter barked.

"Not bullshit. True. When Jay had his mouth on you, you went wild. You couldn't control yourself."

Hunter eyed her warily.

"You know I'm right," she told him. "Think about it. The first time his lips touched your cock, something told you it was different. You loved it. In fact, when he stopped you yelled at him not to."

"I yelled at *you*."

"But I wasn't touching you. Jay was. And when he continued you went out of your mind. You couldn't hold off. He had you so turned on, so aroused, you came in his mouth. Jay's mouth, not mine."

"Goddammit," Hunter exploded. "I thought it was yours."

Before she could respond, a second masculine voice spoke up.

"What's upsetting you, Blondie?" Jay asked. "The fact that a man had your dick in his mouth, or the fact that you liked it?"

Hunter's eyes narrowed to dangerous slits as he glared at Jay. His cheeks turned beet red. "Fuck you, Baxter."

"Fuck me, or fuck you?" Jay asked, his voice sharp. "Which

one do you really want?"

"I want you to get the hell out of my house and not come back. Ever."

"Hunter," Julia gasped. "You don't mean that."

"You bet I do!"

"Yeah, see, I also don't believe you mean that," Jay taunted. "I think what you want is for me to take your dick again and give it another stupendous blowjob." Jay walked forward so Julia could now see he wore a pair of boxers and nothing else. "Or maybe," he continued, his gaze fixed on Hunter, his mouth grim, "maybe you want your own mouthful of man juice. Maybe you want to try blowing me."

If possible, Hunter's cheeks turned even redder. "Don't push me, Jay. I'll kick your sorry ass out of the door faster than you can blink."

Jay raised an eyebrow. "So that's what you want to do with my ass? Kick it?" He snickered in obvious disbelief. "Mate, after the quality of that blowjob, I think there's a lot more you want to aim at my ass than your foot."

Julia's jaw dropped open.

Hunter's chair crashed to the floor. He was on his feet and advancing on Jay at killer speed.

"Hunter. No!" She grabbed his arm, trying to yank him to a halt. Her shoulder about jerked out of her socket before Hunter reacted to her anxiety and stopped.

"I'm sorry, Jules," he said without looking at her. He stared daggers at Jay. "But you need to let me go. Now."

Damn it, so much testosterone flooded the room there was only one way this argument was going to end. With someone lying on the floor, injured. While Jay might be taller than Hunter, Hunter was broader. It was anyone's guess who'd be the first man down.

Jay stood a little straighter. "No worries, Jules. You can drop your hold on him."

Not a chance. The muscles bulged in Hunter's arm, warning Julia he was preparing to throw the first punch.

"See, he's not going to hurt me," Jay explained as he stared straight back at Hunter. "He doesn't want a fight. He wants...this."

To Julia's flabbergasted surprise, Jay flashed Hunter. Even from five odd paces away, she could see the way Jay's cock stood proud and erect. Good God, he was turned on. With all the craziness going on around them, he was aroused.

Before she had a full second to process her thoughts, Hunter had ripped free of her grasp and leapt at Jay. He landed against him with a sickening thud. The force of his attack sent them both crashing to the floor. Jay landed on his back, spread-eagle. Hunter landed on top of him.

Hunter pulled back, lifted his arm and clenched his hand into a fist. He looked murderous.

If his hand connected with Jay's nose, he'd break it.

Jay said something in a voice so soft Julia couldn't hear. But Hunter did and he froze. He relaxed his hand then clenched it into a fist again. Then relaxed it.

Julia dropped to her knees, closer to the men. When Jay spoke again, she heard him.

"It's what you want, Miles."

"No, Baxter." Hunter's hand formed the fist again. Muscle strained in his back and neck. "What I want is to smash your teeth in."

Again Jay spoke too softly to hear.

"Never," Hunter roared and his arm flashed through the

air.

Before his fist met its target, Jay flipped them both. This time Hunter landed on his back, with Jay on top of him, pinning his body down with his chest and holding his arms with his hands. They were inches away from Julia.

"You're lying," Jay snapped. "You want it as much as I do."

"I want Jules, you stupid fuck. Not you." Hunter panted as Jay pressed his weight on his chest.

"Then why do you have a massive hard-on?"

Hunter bared his teeth. "It's adrenaline, asshole. I'm about to beat the shit out of you, and I'm excited by the thought."

Jay shook his head. "You want to fuck the hell out of me, dickhead."

"It's Jules I want to fuck. You I'm gonna beat to a bloody pulp."

"You want to fuck both of us."

To Julia's astonishment, Jay twisted his hips, as though dry-humping Hunter.

"Fuck you," Hunter bellowed.

"As you wish," Jay shot back and dropped his head fast.

For the second time in minutes Julia stared slack-jawed. Jay crushed his mouth over Hunter's in what could only be a bruising kiss.

Hunter froze for a second before roaring back to life. Sheer brute force must have motivated him. Jay lay like a dead weight on top of him, yet in a blur of motion the men rolled a second time, and once again Hunter was on top. "Goddamn you, Jay," he snarled.

And then his lips were on Jay's, his tongue pushing for entrance into the other man's mouth. The kiss looked like a violent scuffle, or a nasty battle of wills, and Julia feared one of them might do permanent damage to the other.

But Hunter gave a small moan, and the fight seemed to ebb out of him. His arms relaxed and the tension in his back visibly slackened. Any violent undertones dissipated in the air around the two men.

Julia watched, gobsmacked, as Hunter's mouth began to seduce rather than attack, as Jay's arms wrapped around Hunter's back and his hands traced the outline of his spine and shoulders. She watched as the kiss transformed into a seductive sharing of passion rather than a lethal end to a friendship.

Jay was right. Hunter *did* want him.

Had he wanted Jay all along?

Julia was struck dumb, barely able to process the scene transpiring before her eyes. The two men she loved and lusted after were engaged in a blistering, all-consuming kiss that upped the room temperature by a good hundred degrees. And damned if it didn't turn her knees to jelly. The carnal, animalistic passion that sizzled between them set her heart racing.

The kiss brought out every forbidden fantasy she'd never had about what the three of them could do together. It also brought out unchecked panic. Jay kissed Hunter. Hunter kissed Jay. There were no inhibitions, there was no holding back. The attraction between the two pulsated through the room, stunning her. *Excluding her.* The men kissed each other. Focused on each other. Neither of them looked at her.

In the midst of all the sexual tension and wanting, Julia felt isolated. Alone. And terrified that now she'd discovered she wanted their threesome more than anything, it was all about to be ripped out from under her for a completely different reason.

An indeterminate amount of time passed before the kiss

ended. Julia's heart pounded. With desire and with fear. Hunter pulled away, breathing heavily. He rolled off Jay and lay beside him on his back, staring at the ceiling.

Jay's now empty arms dropped to the floor. His chest heaved in time to Julia's own racing heart.

"Jesus," Hunter murmured.

Jay gave a soft laugh. "Not quite what you were expecting, huh?"

"Not anything like I expected." Hunter sounded and looked shocked.

Their deep, rasping pants filled the air.

For a solid week Julia had been the center of Jay and Hunter's attention. They'd devoted themselves to pleasing her, to pleasuring her. Now they didn't even notice her. Her stomach twisted in knots. Her lungs seized, and an uncontrolled gasp escaped her mouth.

Hunter twisted around to look at her. His beautiful brown eyes smoldered. But not for her. "Jules?"

"Uh, hi," she said, her voice sounding as tentative as she felt.

He reached out and took her hand. "Hi yourself."

She swallowed. "You okay?"

Hunter's cheeks were red and his expression guarded. He looked at her, then at Jay. Jay grinned up at the ceiling.

"I...I'm not sure," Hunter said when he looked back at her.

Jay's sexy beam vanished.

She nodded. "You look kind of surprised."

He squeezed her hand. "Fuck, Jules. I'd convinced myself you were the only one I wanted."

What? Did that mean he'd thought about being with Jay

before now?

She smiled at him, attempting to beat down the panic. "After what I just witnessed, I'm betting Jay's the only one you want."

Hunter's response was lightning quick. He tugged her hand, hard, and she tumbled forward, landing half on Hunter and half on the floor. He pulled her fully on top of him. Even with his jeans on, Julia couldn't mistake the rigid length of his erection pressing against her belly.

"Do not ever think I don't desire you," Hunter told her. "*Ever*. I spent four months having wet dreams about you. Jerking off to Julia fantasies. Four months wanting you and not touching you because I knew Jay felt the same way. Now that I have you, sweetheart, I'm not letting go." A muscle twitched in his cheek. "Regardless of what Jay and I may or may not do."

Julia buried her face in Hunter's shoulder. Relief swept through her as his words hit home. Not only did Hunter still want her, he wasn't going anywhere either. He was staying right here with her—and with Jay.

It took a good minute or two before she allowed the panic to subside a little and she could talk again. But her fear hadn't abated altogether. Jay hadn't offered her the same reassurances Hunter had.

"What might you and Jay do?" she asked.

"Whatever he'll let me do." It was Jay who answered this time. "Whatever you'll let us do."

Julia turned her head to face him. He'd rolled over and was looking intently at her. "W-whatever I'll let you do?" Her heart banged painfully against her ribs. "What do I have to do with y-you and Hunter?"

"Everything, baby. Don't you see? We're both here because of you. When Hunter finally made his move on you, he opened the door for me to make my move too." Jay grinned at her. "Damn it, woman, don't you know I've been in love with you since forever?"

She gaped at him, unable to say a single word.

His smile dimmed. "Uh, this is the part when you go, 'I love you too, Jay.'"

It was her turn to grin. "I love you too, Jay." She spoke now without hesitation.

His smile came back, bigger than before, and the two of them grinned at each other like lovesick fools.

Hunter cleared his throat.

Julia rested her chin on his chest and looked at him, bolstered by Jay's admission. "I love you too, Blondie."

He ran his hand through her hair. "Yeah? Well that's good, because I'm pretty crazy about you."

She had no doubt Hunter meant every word he said, but his expression concerned her. He looked...haunted. "I would have jumped your bones the first night I met you—if Jay hadn't been there. The two of you have had me in a tizzy these last months, wanting you both and thinking I couldn't have either of you because then I'd have to choose one over the other."

"Far as I'm concerned you can have us both," Jay said. "You don't have to choose."

"I'm good with that," Hunter concurred, and Julia felt a sense of contentment settle over her. Both men loved her.

"Hunter?" Jay said.

"Yeah?"

"Far as I'm concerned *you* can have us both too."

Hunter lay still. His heart raced unevenly beneath her breast.

"Christ, what is it with you two and silence whenever I speak openly," Jay snapped.

Hunter took a deep breath beneath her. "Mate, I appreciate your honesty. I do." He squeezed Julia tight, as though seeking courage from her. "I...I'm just not ready for more than that blowjob yet."

It was Jay's turn to remain silent.

Julia pressed her hand to Hunter's cheek. "Will you ever be ready?"

Hunter grimaced. "Uh, I don't know."

Jay inhaled sharply.

"The thing is...it's all new to me. Too new." Hunter looked at Jay. "Whatever just happened between us, whatever it means—" Hunter tripped over his words. "I need time to wrap my head around it."

"How much time?" Jay asked.

"I'm not sure," he admitted. "Maybe a day, maybe a month. Maybe more, maybe less."

"Yeah, that's real specific, mate."

"Jay," Hunter said, and Julia could hear from his voice that he was deadly serious. "You were right when you said I, er, wanted you. I...do. But the realization is fucking with my head." He shuddered. "This isn't who I am, it's not what I do."

"You're the same person you were an hour ago," Jay told him. "Wanting to be with a man doesn't change that."

Hunter seemed preoccupied. "Yeah, it does." He hugged Julia tight, then hoisted her off him. Waiting only to see she sat comfortably, he stood and began to pace around the room.

"Hunter—" Julia began. She'd never seen him like this, all agitated and upset.

He cut her off. "This changes everything. It changes my

perception of myself and of my past." He looked horrified. "Jesus, it changes my whole fucking life."

Jay sat up. "Mate, kissing a guy doesn't alter the world."

"Oh, really?" Hunter careened to a halt. "That hasn't been my experience."

"Kissing me changed your life?" Jay raised an eyebrow.

"You're not the guy I'm talking about." Hunter's eyes glazed over.

Jay gawked at him.

"You've kissed another man?" Julia asked, scarcely able to believe her ears.

"He wasn't a man." Hunter's voice was hollow. "He was just a kid. We both were. Barely teenagers." He closed his eyes. Pain was etched across his face.

A long silence followed.

Jay opened his mouth to speak, but Julia looked at him and shook her head. Hunter was lost in his memories of another place and time, and she didn't want to disturb him. Whatever he was thinking about, it was deeply personal. If he cared to share it with them, he'd do so at his own pace.

She shuffled closer to Jay, and he wrapped his arm around her. They waited, both watching Hunter. Jay tensed beside her, his muscles flexing as though he wanted to reach out to the other man. Julia ached for Hunter, for whatever unknown hurt he held inside.

"He walked in on us." Hunter didn't open his eyes. Nor did he elaborate.

"Who did?" Jay asked softly.

"My father." The lack of emotion in his voice troubled Julia. "He kicked Scott out, threatened to kill him if he ever stepped foot in our house again." Hunter barked out a harsh laugh.

"Scott never said another word to me. Never even looked in my direction."

"I'm so sorry," Julia whispered.

"I can't blame him. My father's a scary son of a bitch."

"Did he frighten *you*?" she asked cautiously.

"Shitless." Hunter nodded, but still he spoke with no emotion. "After he threw Scott out, he came back to my room and closed the door." Hunter took a deep breath. "He took off his black leather belt and whipped me eight times with it." He rubbed his butt cheek absentmindedly. The same cheek that bore a long, thin, faded scar. "Eight times. With the buckle end of the belt."

Julia sat frozen to the spot, too appalled to respond.

A fierce growl emanated from deep in Jay's chest.

She'd asked Hunter about the scar. He'd avoided answering, saying something about a stupid childhood accident.

"He called me twisted. Abnormal. Swore that no son of his would grow up a screaming queen. Accused me of disgracing him and his family name. He told me *fags* were an anomaly, an abomination." Hunter shrugged. "I believed him."

Loathing rose in Julia's chest. She'd never met his father, but she hated him with every fiber of her being.

"He was wrong," Jay said from between clenched jaws. The rage in his eyes matched her fury.

"Not in the mind of a thirteen-year-old boy," Hunter disagreed. "I was confused anyway, not sure whether I liked guys or girls. My father set me straight." He gave an empty laugh. "Literally."

"Give me five minutes alone with the fucker," Jay murmured under his breath.

"Stand in line," Julia muttered. Christ, and she thought she'd have trouble when her parents found out about her threesome. Hunter's horror story made her fears pale to nothing in comparison.

"I never kissed another guy," Hunter said. "Until now."

Jay swore out loud. He was on his feet before Julia registered he'd moved. Hunter watched him approach, his gaze guarded. Jay didn't flounder. He reached Hunter, opened his arms and pulled the other man into his embrace.

Hunter flinched, but Jay didn't release him. Instead he held him tighter, closer.

The tendons in Hunter's neck bulged, revealing his stress and his indecision.

Jay whispered in his ear.

Hunter's shoulders slumped.

Jay whispered again, and after a moment Hunter nodded.

Jay stroked his back.

Hunter's shoulders went rigid. He tried to pull away.

"Please stay." Jay's voice was hoarse. "Let me help you."

Seconds passed. Hunter remained in Jay's embrace. He even leaned into his friend as though imbibing his touch, his support, but his arms hung limp at his sides.

Julia could stand it no longer. She had to join her men. Hunter's ragged breath echoed through her as she stepped behind him, wound her arms around his waist, and pressed in close against him. "Let both of us help you."

He pushed back, molding himself to her body.

Jay moved his hands to rest on her shoulders and hugged both Julia and Hunter tight. Together Jay and Julia held Hunter for a very long time.

Finally Hunter spoke. "I never kissed another guy." His voice was hoarse as he repeated his earlier confession.

Julia's heart broke for him.

"Until now." The tenderness in Jay's gaze filled Julia with love.

Hunter nodded.

"You've also never fucked a guy," Jay said.

Hunter didn't respond.

Jay dropped a light kiss on Hunter's neck then whispered in his ear. "When you're ready, I'd be honored to be your first."

A violent tremor shook Hunter.

Julia stood on her tiptoes and kissed Jay's cheek.

"And I'd be honored if you were there with us," Jay told her. "Together we can show Hunter that making love with someone you desire is neither an abomination nor an anomaly."

"I'd like that," she answered, her voice thick with unshed tears. "But only if you'd be okay with it, Blondie."

"I...I'm..." Hunter cleared his throat. "Whatever Jay and I do, I'd want you with us, Jules. You know that. But please. Give me time on this issue. Both of you."

"As much as you need, mate," Jay reassured him.

"We'll give you *whatever* you need to get past what your father did and said to you," Julia promised.

"Anything," Jay agreed, and then gently as could be, he covered Hunter's mouth with his own.

The groan that Hunter released resonated with sorrow and pain.

Julia rested her head on Hunter's back and prayed Jay's lips had begun a process that would eventually heal their lover's pain.

Chapter Seven

"You sure you don't want to go out somewhere and watch the fireworks?" Hunter asked, looking out the window.

"I'm more than content where we are," Julia answered. They were spending New Year's Eve at Jay's flat. It had a stunning view of the Harbour Bridge, making it an ideal place to enjoy the New Year festivities. They'd already watched the nine o'clock fireworks from the balcony. The midnight show promised to be even more impressive.

"I'm happy to stay in too." Jay shifted down the couch where seconds earlier she'd been cuddled up to him. "No way I could strip Jules naked if we were out somewhere in public."

Most of her clothes were already scattered around the lounge room. Her glasses, T-shirt, jeans and bra were already off, and Jay was just getting started on her panties. It never failed to amaze Julia how quickly Jay could divest her of her clothing—or how cloudy her reasoning became when his talented hands went to work.

Hunter turned to them in amused silence.

"Ya know I could strip you naked too, don't you?" Jay asked him before he latched onto the strap of her black lace panties with his teeth.

"I know." Hunter nodded.

Julia's heart swelled with love for both of them. Jay had stripped Hunter naked twice since Hunter's story had come out.

The first time, Julia had held Hunter's hand tight as Jay undressed him. When nervous shudders wracked Hunter's body, she'd soothed him with words of love and affirmation. As Jay slid his lips and tongue over Hunter's dick, Julia warded off his fears with a tender kiss. When Hunter's eyes glazed over, and she realized he was getting lost in his memories and doubts of his past, Julia had hauled him back to the present. She'd pressed his hand to her pussy and shown him how much the two men's actions affected her. How incredibly aroused she was watching Jay blowing Hunter.

She'd kept his hand there, guiding it to her clit so she could rub herself against him. And when Hunter had finally won his battle with his misguided conscience and erupted in Jay's mouth, she'd come on his fingers.

The second time had been less emotionally taxing for all of them. Hunter was more relaxed, more accepting of his desire for Jay. So when Jay dropped his head in Hunter's lap, Julia joined him in his feast. Together they'd brought Hunter to a spectacular orgasm.

It was a slow process, but Hunter was overcoming his fear of his father and conquering his misconceptions of his desire for men. Gradually he was admitting to himself and to them that he liked men as much as he did women. More specifically, he'd confessed his desire for Jay equaled his lust for Julia. His willingness to let Jay in, in the face of his past, made him the bravest man she'd ever met. And Jay's gentleness and understanding made her adore him even more.

She giggled as Jay tossed her panties over the back of the couch and licked a sensitive spot on her upper left thigh. "Come closer, Blondie," she summoned Hunter, delighted by the lightheartedness of his mood. "I'll strip you, and Jay can lick us both."

"Or you could both lick me," Jay suggested and planted a tiny kiss on her hip.

Hunter growled.

A shiver of anticipation swept up Julia's spine. Would Hunter do that again? Last night, sitting tentatively beside Julia, Hunter had taken Jay's cock in his mouth and given him head for the first time.

He'd begun with awkward licks and uncertain sucks, but his confidence—and erection—had grown as Jay responded with loud moans and uncontrolled spasms. Within minutes, Hunter had lost himself in his task. As he'd told Julia later, he'd simply done to Jay what he enjoyed having done to himself. And if Jay's thunderous shout of release had been anything to go by, he'd enjoyed it too.

The sight of Hunter blowing Jay had Julia so turned on that the second Jay came she'd impaled herself on Hunter's dick. The two of them hadn't lasted a minute.

Jay sat up and ran a finger through the folds of her pussy. Julia sighed at the delicious sensations his touch evoked.

"Both of us licking you is a thought," Hunter said noncommittally.

Jay looked at Hunter. "Would you rather fuck me?"

Julia caught her breath.

Hunter didn't reply.

"Miles?" Jay prompted, and there was a not-so-subtle change to the air around them.

It took a few seconds for Hunter to answer. "I-I've never considered making love to a man before you." His voice was raw with emotion.

Goosebumps broke out on Julia's skin. Hunter hadn't spoken about fucking or sex. He'd used the words making love, and Julia was pretty sure they were a deliberate choice.

Jay did not have a quick comeback or a cheeky grin. He simply stared at Hunter. Julia couldn't let Hunter's statement pass unacknowledged, nor could she let him carry the load of the conversation. It was too heavy for a man with such a tortured past.

"Have you ever made love to another man, Jay?" she asked.

Jay shook his head. "No." His voice was husky. "I...I've been with other men, but..." He looked up at Hunter. "But it was never about love."

Julia's breath caught in her throat.

Hunter stumbled backwards until he found the other couch and collapsed into it. "Jay..."

"Blame Jules," he told Hunter, his voice still not quite normal. "It's her fault. I watched her watching you for four months."

"You watched me?" Julia blustered. "But...but that would mean you knew I had the hots for Hunter."

"Of course I knew." Jay stroked her clit again, making her moan from the exquisite sensations. "You drooled every time you looked at him."

"She drooled when she looked at you, Jay," Hunter corrected. His voice was deep and sexy. "It made me jealous as hell."

So much for her brilliant bluffing technique. She bent her knee to allow Jay better access. "I drooled over both of you. A lot." She still did. "What's your point, Jay?"

He drew his finger through her slick folds. "It made me wonder what you saw when you looked at Hunter," Jay said, his gaze focused between Julia's legs. "So I started watching him too." He shrugged and color rose in his cheeks. "Now I know," he whispered.

"I saw a man I fell in love with a little more every day. A man I desperately wanted to make love with," Julia told Jay. Her voice was lower than usual. Arousal made it difficult to talk.

Jay's smile was shy. He turned to look at Hunter. "That's pretty much what I saw."

Hunter didn't answer. At all. In fact the silence stretched out for so long, Julia began to get edgy. "It's too quiet," she said. "Why haven't you said anything, Blondie?"

It was Jay who answered. "Sometimes words aren't necessary."

"What does that mean?" She peered at the couch, but Hunter sat too far away for her to see him clearly. His hands were moving near his lap, but his face was a blur.

Jay gave a small laugh. "Ah, for a minute there I forgot you weren't wearing your glasses." His voice was thick with repressed passion. He dipped his finger inside her, pushing it deep into her channel and then out again. "Hunter's looking at us, baby. He's unbuttoning his pants." Jay shuddered. His tone dropped a notch, and he buried his finger inside her once more. "He's looking at us and stroking himself at the same time."

Blood rushed to Julia's head. Sweet, hot desire rose in her body. She squeezed her inner muscles around Jay's finger. "Do you think Hunter saw in us what we saw in him?"

Again Jay nodded. "I suspect he did."

"Hunter," Julia said softly, arching her hips so Jay could penetrate her deeper. "Did you fall in love with us a little more every day?"

Hunter spoke in a voice mellowed with lust and emotion. "Ah, Four Eyes. I've loved you since day one. You should know that by now."

"And you desperately want to make love to me?"

"More desperately every time I see you," Hunter confirmed.

Julia melted inside. "How about Jay?"

"I wanted Jay all along." This time his voice was tinged with something else. Trepidation? "But I couldn't admit it."

"You're admitting it now," Julia said softly.

"It's becoming easier to acknowledge."

"Are you ready to act on your acknowledgement?" Jay asked. Julia could hear the anticipation in his question.

Hunter let out a long breath. "Not yet."

Jay sighed. "Pity," he said. "Because watching you pull on your dick like that..." He let his words trail off.

"You know what I'd really like?" Hunter asked.

"Tell us," Julia invited.

Hunter's answer reverberated down her spine, sending tentacles of desire snaking through her. "I want to watch Jay make love to you."

Holy moly. That sounded both wicked and delicious. Julia squirmed on the couch as her body tightened at the thought.

"And what'll you do?" Jay asked. If he was disappointed the conversation had moved away from Hunter making love to him, he didn't show it.

"What I'm doing now. I'll sit right here and...passively observe."

The pregnant pause told Julia there was nothing passive about his actions. His hand was still on his shaft, and he still stroked himself.

Jay put his hand on his dick and adjusted himself. His erection was clear even in his shorts. "Sounds..." Jay's voice broke. "Sounds...good to me. Y-you okay with that, baby?"

"Mmm. You bet." She squirmed again. "But..."

His eyes darkened and he pumped his finger inside her pussy. She hissed out a breath of air. "But what?"

"No more foreplay. Please. I'm too horny. I won't make it through any...extra attention." Heck, she was about ready to come right now. Between all the talk of love, Jay's caresses and his open desire for Hunter to fuck him, Hunter's request to watch Jay make love to her and the image of Hunter masturbating, she doubted she'd last very long. "Just love me."

Jay bolted upright. "I need a condom."

"Right here." With a soft rustle, something shot through the air, coming from Hunter's side of the room. Jay caught it in one hand.

"One more thing, Four Eyes," Hunter said. "Put your glasses on. I want you to see what watching both of you does to me. What it's always done to me, even though I never admitted it."

Julia didn't have to be told twice. She grabbed her glasses as Jay stripped and sheathed himself. It was difficult to decide where to look first—at Jay standing naked by the couch, proud and erect. Or at Hunter sitting on the sofa opposite, with his jeans crumpled at his feet as he indolently pulled on his dick.

Again dizziness suffused her. Her two lovers made her giddy. And happy. And very, very horny.

"Come sit here, Jules," Jay instructed as he patted the couch. "Slouch down low and put your butt on the edge of the cushion. Yep, that's it." He knelt on the floor in front of her. "Now, spread your thighs, wide." He watched as she drew her legs apart, his breath coming in short, sharp pants. "Christ,

222

yeah. Just like that." His eyes dilated. "Fuck, Miles. She's so wet. So...inviting."

"Do it, Jay," Hunter said in a shaky voice. "Fuck her while I watch."

"Do it," Julia repeated, encouraging Jay. She lifted her legs higher.

Jay groaned and leaned into her. "Wrap your legs around me, baby. Let me in."

Their lips met as Julia's feet touched Jay's lower back. And just like that he slipped inside her. For endless moments they kissed. Neither moved. Perhaps each sensed the other would lose control if Jay drove into her now. God knew Julia was hanging on by a thread.

Jay broke the kiss and rested his forehead against hers. Julia counted to twenty, willing herself to relax. Slowly, slowly, the urgency passed. Slowly, slowly, Jay began to move. With the need to orgasm pushed to the side for now, Julia began to respond. Without haste she rolled her hips to meet Jay's thrusts, loving the feel of him all snug inside her, loving the friction of his penis against her slick flesh, loving *him*.

Hunter moaned.

Julia looked over Jay's shoulder. Hunter's gaze was fixed on the two of them, his expression hazy with desire. He'd stopped stroking himself and instead held his shaft in a firm grip.

"Do you like what you see?' Julia asked, knowing he did.

"I love it. I love seeing you all hot like that. With your legs wrapped around Jay and your pussy clasping him tight. Christ, it's beautiful. You're beautiful."

A fresh gush of moisture pooled in her pussy.

Jay groaned with pleasure. "Damn, baby. Did Hunter do

that to you?"

"Yes." She struggled to speak. "Listening to him. Watching him...watching us. Hot!"

Jay twisted round to look at Hunter and growled deep in his throat.

Hunter's voice was sexy as sin. "I'm watching you too, Jay."

Jay gasped, and Julia could have sworn his cock grew another inch inside her.

Hunter tugged on his dick again. "I've watched you for a long time. Knowing I couldn't have you never stopped me from wanting you. I...I thought that watching would be the closest I ever came to touching you."

A low groan escaped Jay. "Hunter, Christ!" He thrust hard, then froze, remaining deep inside her. "You can touch me whenever you feel like it. Jesus, I want you to touch me."

His dick filled her, satisfied her. She gloried in its length and thickness.

Hunter pumped his cock faster. "How about you, Jules?" he asked in a gruff voice. "Do you want me to touch Jay?"

"God, yes," she cried. She took a deep breath, steadied her pulse and said in measured words, "I want you to make Jay feel the same way he's making me feel now. The way you make me feel."

"How do you feel?" Hunter asked.

There weren't enough words to convey her answer. "Treasured, beautiful, aroused, awestruck, loved."

Jay kissed her. "You are loved, baby."

"Show her," Hunter urged. "Show us both how much she means to you."

Jay's low moan echoed through the room. He pulled out and plunged back into her. She squeezed her legs around his waist, holding him tight so she didn't lose her grip. Lord, she never wanted to let go of him.

She and Jay made love. The sensations he stirred within had her floating on a cloud of delicious desire.

Time lost meaning. Light and dark merged. All Julia focused on were the exquisite tingles chasing their way through her pussy and up her spine. Her eyes closed and she lost herself to Jay's hypnotic, delectable rhythm, knowing Hunter watched every move, every action, and enjoyed it just as much as they did.

A shudder rippled through Jay, knocking her out of tempo. Sluggishly Julia opened her eyes, and her heart skipped a beat.

Hunter stood behind Jay. His legs must have been spread wide because he stood lower than usual. One hand rested on Jay's back, the other she couldn't see. He bit his lower lip as though in agony, and his gaze was fixed on Jay's butt.

Jay shuddered again and jerked into Julia.

She bit back a moan. "What's he doing, Jay?" she asked, her voice nothing more than a whisper.

"T-touching me." Jay's eyes were closed. He'd stilled inside her.

Goosebumps ran over her arms. "H...how?" God, she could barely talk.

"Fingers," Jay murmured. "Sliding over me." He took a shaky breath. "In me."

Her mind filled with graphic images and she couldn't stop the husky moan that escaped. "How does it feel?"

"Almost...as good...as you...do. *Oh, fuck!*" He drove into her.

Julia clenched her inner muscles and tried not to pass out from pleasure. "What? Tell me."

"Added...another finger," he panted. A tiny frown creased

his forehead.

"Is it painful?" she asked.

"No. It's fucking incredible."

She gazed at Hunter. His lips were parted and his eyes hooded. He looked as though he couldn't believe what he was doing. He also looked as though he couldn't stop doing what he was doing.

"Hunter." She breathed his name.

He glanced up and smiled at her; a smile that hinted at love, desire and frustration.

Julia caught her breath. "H-how many fingers?"

"Two," Jay said.

Hunter shook his head. "Three," he corrected as Jay jerked again.

This time there was no doubting the crease on Jay's forehead was caused by pain.

"It's okay," Julia whispered. She stroked his cheeks and repeated the very words Jay had once soothed her with. "Take a minute to get used to the stretch." Then she added a few of her own. "It'll be worth it, I swear."

Hunter said nothing, but the look he gave her scorched her all the way through to her bones, setting fire to places Jay had yet to touch.

Seconds passed. Jay breathed. *In, out. In, out.*

Hunter breathed too, more heavily than Jay.

The frown disappeared, along with the tension in Jay's shoulders. He began thrusting into her again, setting off all sorts of wonderful sensations inside Julia. But his rhythm was off, as if his focus was incomplete.

Again Hunter looked at her, this time with an exultant

expression.

A cry of frustration broke free from Jay. "Goddammit, Hunter. I want your dick, not your fingers."

"I—" Hunter breathed hard. "I want...your ass."

Julia grew lightheaded all over again. Hunter's admission had taken an enormous amount of courage.

Jay panted, the lust in his face blinding.

She wanted Hunter in Jay's ass almost as much as Jay did. But... "Are you okay doing this, Blondie?" Hunter had to be sure. If he wasn't, his next move could blow his confidence and their relationship right out of the water.

Hunter licked his lips. "I've made love to you, Jules. Now I want—need—to make love to Jay. To...both...of you."

She smiled and nodded, or tried to anyway, but blood rushed to her head and dizziness swamped her.

Jay made a funny sound in the back of his throat, wrenching Hunter's attention away from her. Hunter moved his hand off Jay's back and looked down.

Heavy breathing filled the air. Julia had no idea whose it was. Probably all three of theirs.

There was movement behind Jay, but much as she wanted to know, she couldn't see what was happening. Then Jay gulped. He opened his eyes and stared at her. His pupils were tiny pinpricks, his irises glazed with lust. "Jules. Oh, fuck. *Jules.*" His voice was wanton and husky, and he shifted inside her in uncoordinated movements.

"Jay!" Hunter's eyes were scrunched closed, and his head was tilted back. Drops of perspiration beaded on his upper lip. He rested one hand on Jay's waist and the other he wrapped around her leg, connecting them all. His touch was intimate and erotic.

"Deeper," Jay rasped. A second later he jerked inside Julia again.

It was Julia's turn to gasp as a loud bang echoed through the room. Oh, sweet Lord. Good God. It was happening. Jay was making love to her, and Hunter was making love to Jay. All at the same time.

"Fuck!" Jay yelled. "I'm seeing fireworks." This time when he jerked inside her, Julia couldn't contain her cry of delight.

Hunter gasped. "Rockets...going off in my head...too." His fingers skimmed over the sensitive skin of her calf. "Fuck, Jay, I'm buried balls-deep in your ass."

The room exploded in a multitude of colors.

"It's midnight," Julia panted, realizing she too was seeing fireworks. The night sky was ablaze. Dazzling flashes of light illuminated the horizon. Thunderous booms reverberated through her body.

The three lovers absorbed their situation. Hunter stared at Julia, while Jay knelt in front of him, captivated. The fireworks outside were brilliant, an ideal complement to the pyrotechnics inside the flat.

"It's perfect," Julia said at last. "The perfect way to welcome in the New Year." And Hunter was responsible for making it so. He amazed her. His desire for her and Jay had helped him overcome his father's vicious taunting. He'd put his fears and doubts aside to complete their threesome.

Her heart raced. *Their threesome was complete.* Apart they were three separate entities. Together, like this, they became a whole.

Hunter's smile was slow to form. "Yeah, Four Eyes, it sure is."

Julia smiled back at Hunter. "You really do love Jay, don't

you?"

Jay's breath caught.

Hunter's smile grew. He nodded.

She smiled back.

"As much as I love you," he said.

"I love you too."

Fireworks exploded around them.

At which point Jay surged into her with unbridled zeal. Both she and Hunter gasped as Jay lost control. He drove into her, once, twice, a hundred times, the pressure of his thrusts a sublime torture to her pussy.

Hunter also lost his restraint. He pounded into Jay from behind. In minutes the three of them developed a new rhythm. Hunter drove into Jay, forcing him deep into Julia. When Hunter pulled out, Jay followed suit, only to repeat the process as Hunter plunged into him again. The air was rent with noisy blasts and breathless moans. The scent of sex flowed around them, filling her nose.

Julia was on a sexual high the likes of which she'd never dreamed she'd experience. And when Jay let rip with a mighty roar and lost himself to the throes of his orgasm, Julia let reality slip away. All that registered were the increasing tingles filling her pussy, the lights flashing behind her eyelids and the overwhelming need to release the sweet tension building in her loins. As Jay pulsed inside her, Julia's own climax blindsided her. She lost herself to the passion of the moment, and to the beauty and adoration of the men she loved.

Hunter's hoarse cry only increased her pleasure. It pounded through her groin, and washed over every nerve ending in her body. Even when her climax subsided, tiny streaks of pleasure still undulated through her, prolonging the sensation, extending the ecstasy.

As the impact of their lovemaking began slowly to wear off, the colors and sounds outside faded once again to dark silence. It was long moments before any of them could move, let alone talk.

Chapter Eight

"I think it's safe to say we brought in the New Year with a bang," Jay said with a content grin. He pushed himself up on shaky legs and disposed of his condom.

Hunter did the same, then both men collapsed down beside her.

"Happy New Year, Four Eyes." Hunter pressed a kiss to her mouth. Then he turned around and did the same to Jay. "Happy New Year."

Jay then kissed Julia, and minutes or hours later the three of them finally came up for air.

"I think," Julia said sagely, "that this must be what it feels like to be dealt a royal flush."

Jay frowned. "I'm not sure about that. We need to test your theory with another round. Ready to deal the cards, Blondie?"

"Give me a couple of minutes, then ask again."

"How about you, Jules?" Jay asked her.

She took a deep breath. "It's not just a matter of minutes, guys. It's..." She let the words fade away. It was a New Year. She shouldn't ruin the moment. On the other hand, it was New Year's, and what better time was there to make resolutions and sort out concerns?

In seven days Hunter had not only managed to confront his

family issues, he'd begun to conquer them too. She'd been dithering over her fear of introducing Hunter and Jay to her sister and parents for weeks. It was time to take a page out of Hunter's book and face her concerns head on.

She loved two men. And they loved her—and each other. Yes, their relationship might be different from the norm, but that didn't mean it couldn't last. It also didn't mean she should be ashamed of it.

Julia was proud of her men. She was proud of what they'd created together. And she'd be proud to introduce them to her family.

Hunter's gaze was on her. "It's what, Four Eyes?"

She took a deep breath. Hell, they'd come this far. No point beating around the bush now. "I...I don't want to play anymore."

Jay froze. "Whaddya mean?"

"You want out, Jules?" Hunter asked.

"God, no!" Julia said. "I want in. Permanently. That's the thing. I don't want to play games. I want whatever this is between us all to be real. To be a proper, committed relationship." She worried her lower lip. "I'm tired of keeping my feelings for you secret from the world. I love you guys. I'm proud of what we have and..."

Her words dried up. Jay was gaping at her, and Hunter looked dazed.

A sudden wave of nausea hit her. She'd just put herself out there. Revealed her true desires—and she was terrified by their reaction. Did they disagree with her?

"Fuck." Jay's shoulders sagged. "I thought you were about to blow us off."

Hunter let out a long, unsteady breath. "Christ, me too."

Relief plowed into her. "Yeah, well. No." As if she'd be stupid enough to give up the best thing that had ever happened to her. "Just the opposite."

Hunter sat up and leaned against the couch. Again his eyes saw right into her thoughts. "You want to introduce us to your sister, don't you?"

"I do."

"Kim?" Jay asked.

Julia nodded.

Jay scrunched his nose in confusion. "How did you know Jules wants us to meet her?" he asked Hunter. "What have I missed?"

"We spoke about it last week," Hunter told him. "Julia felt awkward about introducing the two of us to Kim as her boyfriends."

"Understandable," Jay mused. "It's not something you get to do every day."

"What made you change your mind?" Hunter asked her.

"You did." Tears filled her eyes. "I've been so worried what my family would say about my sleeping with two men. And then I looked at you, making love to Jay, to both of us, and I was ashamed of myself. If you could rise above the fears your father instilled in you, I can tell my family the truth about the men I love."

She wasn't an idiot. She knew her parents would be shocked by the choices she'd made, by her rejection of their traditional values and expectations. It would be a long while before they felt anywhere near comfortable with her decisions. She'd have to take her time with the introductions. Make them slowly. Kim was the obvious person to start with. Julia knew her sister would get along famously with both men, and with Kim on her side, telling her parents would be a whole lot easier. Heck, sometime in the not-too-distant future she might even tell her great-aunt Edith.

"I didn't get through this alone, Jules," Hunter said. "You and Jay helped me. Every step of the way. So did my mom."

"Your mother?" Jay asked in surprise.

Hunter nodded. "I went to see her today. Well, yesterday. I told her about all of us."

"What did she say?" Jay asked.

"More than I ever expected." Hunter closed his eyes. "It took her years to bring up Scott with me. It was only when I moved out of home that she told me how much she hated what my father had done. For her, it was the beginning of the end of their marriage."

Julia thought about her conversation with Hunter a week ago. He'd said then he and his mother had issues they'd had to work through. Hunter's father and Scott had obviously headed that list.

"Yesterday I surprised her when I explained the nature of our threesome. But she got through it like a trooper. She even gave me her blessing."

"She did?" Julia asked. "Just like that?"

"It took her a while to process everything. But deep down, my mother's a romantic. She wants me to be happy." He was silent a minute. "She's been afraid for a long time that I'd be too scared to find true happiness—because of my father." He smiled. "I think she's rather proud of the fact I've now found two people I love."

"I think I'd like to meet your mother," Julia mused.

"That's a good thing, because she wants to meet you." He looked at Jay. "How about it? You up to meeting her?"

Jay thought for a minute. "Yeah, I'd be happy to. And I'd also like to meet Kim. Hell, Jules speaks about her so often I feel like I already know her."

Julia smiled shyly. "I'd be proud to introduce you to my sister. Both of you."

"Jay?" Hunter turned to him. "What about you? You up to introducing us to your family?"

Jay snickered. "I'm just thinking how I'm going to break the news."

Julia's heart thumped. "Will it be hard for them to hear?" Surely it couldn't be worse than Hunter's father finding out about his son's bisexual tendencies.

"My father almost had a heart attack when my brother told them he was gay. My mother cried for a week. I'm one up on Michael. At least when I introduce them to my male lover it won't be so bad. I'll have a female lover to introduce as well."

"Oh, my God, Jay. Are we putting your father's health at risk by telling him?" Julia asked.

"Nah, Four Eyes." Jay laughed. "I'm overstating the case. It took a while, but my folks are cool with Michael now. I think they'll take to both of you pretty easily."

Again the three of them lapsed into silence, each letting their conversation sink in.

"Wow," Julia said. "We're really going to do this. We're committing to one another, and we're going public with our families."

"It sure looks that way," Jay agreed.

"Talk about starting the New Year with a bang," Julia mused.

"If the rest of this year is anything like the start, I suspect we're in for a mighty good twelve months," Hunter said.

"The best." Jay nodded.

"So you're both sure about this? About us?" Julia asked.

"Babe, far as I'm concerned, it's a no-brainer," Jay said. "Couldn't be more sure."

"Just like that?" Was it that simple? Could everything that had seemed so complicated just a few days ago be this easily resolved?

"Hey, if a short answer isn't enough, I could bring out my trumpet and turn it into a grand announcement," Jay said. "Otherwise, yep. Just like that."

"You too?" Julia asked Hunter, wanting to be one hundred percent sure.

"I could use Jay's trumpet if you'd like."

She smacked his arm. There was a brightness in Hunter's voice that hadn't been there for a while. A buoyancy in his step, a lightness to his stance, as though he no longer carried the weight of the world—or the burden of his father's prejudices—on his shoulders.

"But," Hunter said, and Julia's lungs seized, "if we're going public, does this mean we can't play anymore?"

Julia considered her answer. "So long as what we have is real and committed, there's no reason we can't have fun with it. Heck, yeah, we can play." Julia grinned at him. "In fact, I'm willing to lay a bet on this relationship. If you're up to it, boys, I'm going all in."

"Whaddya say, Miles?" Jay asked. "You up to it?"

Hunter groaned as his dick jerked. "Sure looks that way."

Julia grinned at him. So did Jay.

"I'm in too," Jay said, and crushed his mouth against Hunter's. Minutes later Hunter took Julia's lips in a scorching kiss.

And then they went all in.

About the Author

To learn more about Jess Dee, please visit her website at: www.jessdee.com or her blog at: http://jessdee.wordpress.com. Or send an email to jess@jessdee.com.

Sign up with the Heat Wave Yahoo! group to join in the fun with Jess and other authors and readers at: http://groups.yahoo.com/group/Heat_Wave_Readers.

The voice of an angel, a husband who loved her—she had it all...until a tragedy took it away.

Songbird
© 2009 Maya Banks

They called her their Songbird, but she was never theirs. Not in the way she wanted.

The Donovan brothers meant everything to Emily, but rejected by Greer and Taggert, she turned to Sean, the youngest. He married her for love, and she loved him, but she also loved his older brothers.

Her singing launched her to stardom. She had it all. The voice of an angel, a husband who loved her, and the adoration of millions. Until a tragedy took it all away.

Taggert and Greer grieve for their younger brother, but they're also grieving the loss of Emmy, their songbird. They take her back to Montana, determined to help her heal and show her once and for all they want her. They're also on a mission to help her find her voice again. Under the protective shield of their love, she begins to blossom... until an old threat resurfaces.

Now the Donovans face a fight for what they once threw away. Only by winning it—and her love—will their songbird fly again.

Warning: Explicit sex, ménage a trois, multiple partners, a committed polyamorous relationship, adult language and sweet loving.

Available now in ebook and print from Samhain Publishing.

LaVergne, TN USA
06 January 2011
211398LV00004B/1/P